洞月亮

CAVE MOON PRESS

YAKIMA 中 WASHINGTON

2 0 1 5

AUTISM
isn't a crime

just ask the ghost of Frank Reid

DP JOHNSON

Illustration by: Hayden Sevigny
Book Design: Honeylette Pino and Doug Johnson
Editors: Lynne Greene and Josina Bickel

ISBN: 978-0692490075

Dedicated to Lori Flatland
(1965-2014)

Please forgive any clinical inconsistencies about Autism Spectrum Disorder. This is a work of fiction. All of the characters, names, incidents, organizations, and dialogue in this novel are either the products of the author's imagination or are used fictitiously. A debt of gratitude goes to my dear friend Lori who shared her stories with me and her life with her children. This is written for her, Josh and all the Flatland children. Proceeds benefit various Autistic Awareness organizations including but not limited to the Alaska Autism Resource Center

Chapter 1

I thought she would like the complete works of Shakespeare in her locker. It's a good thing I ducked.

"I wanted to just be friends!" Daphne shrieked as she wound up for the pitch. She threw the book hard. It's not like I was a full blown stalker or anything. I'm not some kind of genius computer hacker. How hard is it to get a locker combination? My name is Rocky. Actually my name is Harold Reginald Blackbear Jones III. Nobody calls me Harry or Reggie like they do Mike. Nobody calls me Harold or Reginald like the substitute does Beauregard. He has to correct them by yelling, "Just Bo!" They call me Rocky because, well, I rock. I didn't really notice it. When I was in first grade, the teacher put me in with the Bluebird reading group before I read a single word on the page. Devlin pointed at me rocking. He snickered his big butt off. My name has been Rocky ever since. I'm not in the first grade now. I'm in the seventh. The teachers still treat me like I am in first. That's when it all started. You'll have to be patient. I mix up my years. I'm going to be a famous crime novelist when I grow up. Mickey Spillane in *Spies from the Crypt* said, "If you are reading this, then I'm dead." That was the key to the mystery. I'm not dead. This isn't the key. I'm just letting you read my notebook. Not everyone gets to read my notebook. I know people use laptops now. I use notebooks. If I get lost, then just wait a little while. My friends know they have to wait. I'll come back. Honest. I remember the important things. One important thing is that I found Frank Reid's diary. Well

1

kind of. Nobody else did. I'm kind of sad because it was a real diary. I can't use it as a famous crime novel because I didn't make it up. I'll make up a better story later. This story starts in first grade. I'm in seventh grade now. This is my story.

I was rocking with the Bluebirds and picking at the binding of the book wondering why the letters were so big when Principal Higgins asked me why I chose to destroy school property. I gave her a blank look, not remembering that earlier in the week I tripped trying to get back to my seat and the page with the smiling elephant came off in my hand. The smiling elephant was in the principal's hand with some other school form.

The principal repeated the question louder like I was deaf, and I said, "Elephants don't smile. Their trunks block the view. The picture looks nothing like you. Mostly because you don't smile either and you don't have a trunk. Billy said you're as big as a house but I told him that's impossible because our house is 1168 square feet, and you don't even come close." She wrinkled her nose and the eyebrow that went all the way across her forehead. My Aunt Beatrice has a mole. She wrinkles that brown fleshy marble with chin hair. She wrinkles it when she calls me a smart—(My Mom Won't Let Me Say That Word=MMWLMSTW.) Sorry. Smarty pants. My Mom says I can't say MMWLMSTW or fart. I have to say bottom or stinker. I told her that MMWLMSTW is also a donkey. They even sing it in church during Christmas. She says that's different. Dad says I'm just a smart MMWLMSTW. Mom doesn't tell him he can't say MMWLMSTW or fart. He has the loudest farts in the whole world. When Dad farts, people think a semi's brakes are gurgling. When Dad farts, people think the moving company is dragging the piano across the floor. My sister and I giggle. Mom frowns. Principal Higgins wrinkles. I was being a smart MMWLMSTW. Sorry. Smarty pants.

You probably think I already lost my place in the story. I kind of did. But that's why I'm writing this down in my notebook. The doctor said that I couldn't just use the meds. She thought writing things down would keep the words from running away all the time. I can always look back and see what I meant to say and try to start over. Teachers forget to tell us that we can look back and see what people are trying to say. It's okay if we start over when we get lost. The principal didn't tell me that on the day I said elephants don't smile. She just sent me home with a note about taking a test.

"Don't slam the door." The silver piston at the top is broken. The screw stripped out in a windstorm. Dad is waiting for a good day to fix it. Mom yells when the screen door slams. The screen door slammed.

"What did you do now, Harold?" My mom called me Harold. She offered me my plate of Oreos at the table. My backpack slid off my shoulder. "Why the big sigh, Detective?" Mom called me Detective instead of Pookums or Sugar like Billy's mom. I'm glad my name is Detective to Mom. I'm going to be a famous crime novelist.

"I tripped, Mom. It wasn't my fault." I was finishing off the bag of Oreos and glass of milk I always had after school. They barely ever fed me anything with the school lunch. I ate it all, but I was always starving when I got home.

"Harold, it's never your fault. What did you do?" she sighed. Mom smelled like pork chops and apple sauce. Mom always smelled like fried food. She was from Texas. She never yelled at me for having accidents at school.

I explained how the Bluebirds all got bored looking at the big letters, and Miss Grundle, the teacher's aide, had to go get her orange vest for playground duty so the kids wouldn't cross the street during afternoon recess and raid the 7-11 on the corner. The only one who did that was Henry Wilson. Henry's dad took him to court so he could tell the judge his uncle wasn't driving drunk on the job. His uncle didn't drink on the job a lot.

"Harold." That was my mom. She reminds me where I am in the story. I daydream a lot. Sometimes she ends up in my notebook where only my friends can look. Make sure you say nice things to her if you see her. She gets tired.

"Right, Mom." Anyway everyone was in a hurry to get out a couple minutes early for recess since Miss Grundle wasn't sure we could read anyway. She wanted to get the special corner of the playground where only girls brought Princess Gwen dolls and made them tap dance on the pavement. The last teacher's aide on the playground always stood next to the swing set and soccer field where boys were always getting the whistle blown to tell them to stop running, pushing and shoving. Mostly the pushing and shoving.

"Harold!"

"It was in Bluebirds. The teacher told us to get ready for recess. I got up and Devlin Monahan stepped on the book right as I tried to pick it up. The page with the giant "E" for elephant came off in my hand.

"Did you tell the teacher?"

"No. She gets upset about the books, and we were in a hurry to go play."

"Did you play with anyone today, Harold?" I wanted to tell Mom that they named me captain of the soccer team. I wanted to tell Mom that they asked me to swing. I wanted to say they let me watch Princess Gwen tap dance on the concrete.

"Had a great time with Lord Dwark. We stalked dragons in the big tractor tires."

"I'll take that as a No."

"Never take No for an answer. That's not the Ameraway." My dad and mom tried to sell vitamins in the evening to try and save for my extra treatments and their anniversary trip to Hawaii. Spouting their sales lines got me off the hook for rocking all by myself in the tires during recess. Well, not all by myself. There was Daphne and a couple other Bluebirds that would play in the sand next to the tire. They didn't have Princess Gwen to tap dance so they just hummed tunes and talked about their dad's weekend.

Daphne was a Robin. I was a Bluebird. She didn't have a Princess Gwen doll, so she played with us. She was lucky enough to make it out but I sat back rocking with the Bluebirds. Her family moved to Anchorage until about a year ago. Her mom came back to help out with the cafe when her grandpa died. Skagway is pretty crazy in the summer. Daphne was even prettier than the first day I saw her as a Bluebird. Devlin was a Bluebird, but his breathe was worse than the first day I met him. Just because I didn't play with anyone didn't mean it stopped people from sitting on my chest and tapping my sternum with their knuckles. But that's getting a little ahead of the story. Mom and Dr. Silverstein say I should try to tell it in order to keep my thoughts from running away. But these are my notebooks. They said I could write however I wanted in my notebook.

Chapter 2

"Lord Dwark."

"Harold, why do you insist on not answering my questions?"

"That's not the Ameraway."

"That's not funny, Harold. I can only sew up so many of your shirts. You need to be more careful." I couldn't see how it mattered. Maybe some kids in seventh grade cared but I don't. My clothes are all piled on my floor. I dress in the dark. Every once and a while my mother snarls and comes in using her broom as a bulldozer. She shoves the pile to one side.

"Pick these up!" she yells. I slink and pick up a t-shirt. My shoulders are shaped like the bicycle racks in front of the library. I wait until she leaves and go back to writing. She hates that. There was this one time I bought a rubber snake to scare my sister Natalie. I scared everybody I could think of with that snake. Adults never flinched, and it's not really fair to scare a first grader when it's your third year in the first grade. I stayed a Bluebird so long because they kept pulling me out of class to take special tests. The teacher said I had to keep the snake at my house. It was still in my pocket from the day before. My pocket was on the pile. My mom, all bulldozer mad, went down to pick up the snake. Only she had already shoved my clothes.

"HAROLD!" Mom shrieked. It was a real garden snake that slithered up through the sewage drain. Until Mom came, it was resting under my Captain America underwear. The pair with the long brown streaks where my butt crack bunches. It slithered again. My mom screamed, and I jumped up on the bed. She stomped back upstairs, so she wouldn't say those words Dad can say but I can't. I was left on my bed until dinner. My room is right next to the washer and dryer room, and we get salamanders all the time. It was the first time I remember seeing a snake. I remember the important things.

"Harold hold still. I'm almost done." Mom didn't stay mad about the snake. That was a while ago. She had me stand on a chair, so she could finish mending my torn shirt. She secretly tried to see how long I could keep from rocking. She was done. "Harold, did you feed Tramp?" I just blinked and groaned. Tramp was my sister Natalie's dog. Feeding the pets was my job. Mom kept a cat named Pickles to keep down the mice. Pickles and Tramp were friends when Tramp wasn't barking at the TV. Tramp was a Pomeranian. Natalie had to clean the bathroom which I thought was a jip because I had to feed them every day. She only had to clean the bathroom on Fridays or when Grandma Corless was coming over. To make it worse, the Pomeranian would even growl at me when I tried to feed him. Tramp yipped and twitched so much I was tempted to give her one of my pills. Then I remembered the story I read where the killer slipped the poison into the dog's food before coming back later to cover his tracks. I didn't want Mrs. Homer, my favorite teacher, to think I was a killer and a retard. She never said it but the way she ignored me said it all. Tramp was jumping up and down and yipping. I thought she was going to throw her hip out from wagging what was left of her tail. She already limped like Grandma Frampton. Dad said we should put her down. I told him we couldn't kill Grandma because she wouldn't be able to bring over those brownies that he likes. He laughed and called me a Smart MMWLMSTW. I scooped some food into the dish, and Tramp nudged me out of the way after growling and wagging her tail. I filled up the automatic water dish that leaked when Tramp kicked it.

Mom lets it go when my mind wanders. Sometimes I just pretend so people will quit talking. She lets me scribble in this notebook. She gets me as many notebooks as I need. So far I'm up to 107. That's a prime number. It's unique because there's only a small mini-series of 101, 103, 107 and 109. Nobody cares. Mom always just says that's nice. Mrs. Homer lets me write in my notebooks and sighs really big when I yell at Devlin for taking my notebooks in the middle of class. Devlin giggles. Even though I'm in seventh and he is in sixth they send us both to Mrs. Homer's class for one period. They say I'm making progress. Dr. Silverstein said I should transition to the real kid classes. Mom says they're going to try to get me to all real kid classes by the time I'm in high school. Maybe by then Daphne will have forgotten that I tried to give her the Shakespeare book. It was just that Daphne told Jessica she loved Shakespeare. Daphne told Jessica her aunt took her to Romeo and Juliet in the park. She was standing three people behind of me in the lunch line one day. I was waiting for them to bring a new tray of steaming peas. The other kids called me a loser and went around me in line. Daphne and Jessica talked so much they didn't notice. I have to eat everything in the lunch they give me, but I'm still hungry all day. Mom feeds me everything I want, but I'm still hungry all day.

Mom says it's not fair that I'm skin and bones and eat so much. That's why it doesn't really matter what I put on in the morning when I get ready. I did start putting my clothes away after the snake slid out from under Captain America's brown streaks. Most all of my clothes were a size or two too large. They came from my cousins. They also gave us an old gaming system and a racing game. I beat the game pretty quick but loved to play. When I started yelling, "Thug Nation Rocks!" every time the video game was reloading my mom said I had to do something else. The game went away. I don't remember the last time I saw clothes that had tags unless it was a piece of masking tape where someone wrote $3 in Sharpie marker. I have green eyes, freckles and that raven black hair that makes everyone wonder about which one of my grandmothers was the Tlingit. Don't worry if you can't pronounce it. You can start your own glossary if you want. Indian Words I Can't Pronounce= IWICP. You can say Native American Words I Can't Pronounce=NAWICP if you want. Dad says it doesn't matter. Your parents might think it matters. Like when we see each other on the street someday. They don't want you to point and call me slow, retarded or weird. They just want you to keep it to yourself. I don't care if you know those other words. They told me I can write what I want in my notebook. I write words in my own glossary I can't call you. Write what you want in your notebook. It's your glossary. Dad named me Blackbear just to cover all the bases even though the tribe wasn't so sure if he was supposed to that.

It used to be a big deal that Dad was Tlingit and Mom was white. Back then we lived in Englewood Heights in Juneau where all the people cut their pretend lawns—not just the old ladies who remembered when this was a nicer neighborhood. We moved to Juneau when Dad lost his job at Ketchikan Spruce Mill. It was when I was three. By the time I started Glacier Valley Elementary, nobody really noticed Mom and Dad. So many people over the years have come up chasing gold, oil or fishing wages that Alaska has pretty much melted together. Devlin's mom was either Puerto Rican or Greek. Daphne was the only freak because both her parents were white. I mean they all cared about it in the news and everything, but when it came down to it, the Bluebirds were all equal. The only time people cared was when someone was a Mallard or an Eagle.

I couldn't tell Mom, but my shirt ripped the usual way. I got caught by Devlin and his goons on the way home. They got me just inside the double doors before I left the school. One goon would watch the teacher's aides all looking the other way at the kids getting on the bus. Then they'd yank my back pack and kick me around a while until Devlin laughed enough to pee. Sometimes a goon would yell, "Someone's coming!" I would just curl up and wait until it was over, hugging my back pack. I didn't care as long as they didn't steal my notebooks.

I like the shirt I was wearing that day. It had huge red stripes liked a *Where's Waldo* book. I pretended I was invisible. I'm pretty skinny but I'm not invisible. If I was invisible, then Devlin couldn't see me. If I was invisible, Mr. Pimpleton wouldn't put a rubber band on my wrist to remind me to stop rocking during Algebra. During homework time I'd just stare out the window, start rocking and he would walk by and snap the rubber band. He read about it in a psychology book. It helped him quit smoking, so when he really cared about a kid he offered him a rubber band. He said he cared. I didn't quit rocking. I told him one day that I might take up smoking and see if the rubber band worked. He said that wasn't funny. I was being a Smart MMWLMSTW.

You can't be invisible. You can't pretend very well either when you're a head taller than the rest of the seventh graders. My dad is tall, and I was a Bluebird for three years instead of one. My first day at Skagway Middle School a kid tried to call me Sherlock Beak. My nose has that big hook you see in the movies. It's my mom's nose. People ask me if I'm Nez Pierce. I don't understand.

"His name is Rocky!" Devlin shouted. He smacked me on the back. My backpack dumped onto the ground. I wish it hadn't taken them so long to give me the tests back in first grade. Things would have been different. When they give you the tests they start putting you in different classes or just do the one on one tutoring thing. If the test would have happened on time my contact with Devlin would have been reduced to recess. There are other kids to pick on out on the playground. With the way things stayed, he could just always snag me on the way out of the door or step on my stuff right before we had to leave. We're way too connected down this way in Alaska. Devlin's dad was a cousin to someone. He was laid off from Ketchikan at the same time as my dad. If I would have escaped first grade earlier and Devlin wouldn't be a character in all those famous crime novels I'm going to write when I'm a grown-up.

Chapter 3

"How did you do on the test?" Back in first grade they told Mom she didn't have to go with me to the test and that a nice lady named Dr. Williams would give them during the school day during my reading time.

"She didn't use any needles."

"What?"

"The doctor said if I had any questions before we started. I asked how much blood they were going to draw."

"Oh, Harold." Mom smelled like tacos that night. Salsa tickled my nose. I would eat it all but it my nose tickled. I got in trouble for sneezing in the salsa. I was always hungry. My sister Natalie wouldn't eat it at all. I got in trouble for rocking. Natalie wouldn't get in trouble for sniffing, sneering and not eating. I tried to be still for Dad but I forgot. Dad got a job as a clerk for a lawyer turned realtor in Skagway. He'd gone to night school when they laid him off from Ketchikan Spruce Mill. The suit and tie made him feel important. When he drank beer on the porch with Uncle George they talked about The Man. The tone in his voice always made me wonder which TV program they watched called The Man. He must have been a dirty-rotten-cheating-son-of-a-MMWLMSTW2-MMWLMSTW3. There are more words my mom won't let me say so I had to start a glossary in the back of my notebooks. She said that when I get to be a famous crime novelist, they won't let me print my glossary. I'm keeping it just in case. All of the chapter books they make me read in school all have a glossary. They put all the hard words in the glossary.

11

Most of Dad's words aren't hard to pronounce. They just follow funny rules. Mom just has rules. The rules don't make sense. Most of the rules in school don't make sense. At least they finally just let me write in my journal and left me alone. Teachers spend hours explaining the rules. They spend hours telling me why the rule is a good idea. They don't understand. The rules swim in my head like fish. Dr. Williams had an aquarium. That's when I figured out the rules are fish. They don't make sense. They just float around all pretty, and they calm people down. By my second year in first grade Dr. Williams found time for me. I'm not sure why I was so hard to find. I wasn't running. I've been a Bluebird the entire time. Even if I wanted to run, everybody knows Bluebirds are slow.

"So how did the test go, Harold? Did you get a high score?"

"Dr. Williams practiced her best doctor poker face, Mom. She told me ahead of time that she was going to compile some report. She told me she wouldn't know for awhile."

"Anything else?"

"She raised her eyebrows when I spelled disambiguation out loud."

"What does that mean, Harold?"

"Clear things up. If a sentence was a dirty window, it would be the Windex."

"Why don't you put that in your glossary?"

"That's a good idea, Mom." So I started two glossaries for when I became a famous crime writing novelist. Disambiguation became the first entry. My glossary won't be in alphabetical order. It's a nice trick they use on use in school, but nobody says it has to be that way. So Disambiguation=My Mom Doesn't Understand That Word=MMDUTW. I label my rules. My rules will be animals at the zoo instead of fish in an aquarium. Animals are pretty, but they don't float around as much. I'll be the zookeeper and feed the animals. My rules will be in boxes for people to look at. They will be pretty like animals.

They kept us Bluebirds together when everyone else went to second grade. Mrs. Martinez changed the name of the groups to colors like Green, Yellow and Red. Everyone knew that the Eagles were green, the Mallards were yellow and the Bluebirds were red. If they weren't sure at the beginning, they were sure by the first recess. Bluebirds lined up five minutes early and were led down to Mrs. Martinez's office to work on reading. Raj moved here from Itasca, New York. Raj said his last name meant his family was really good at making liquor and had even visited the King of England in the 1800's. He said that's why they managed the liquor store. Raj has family members next to the Russians who sell jewelry at the water front. Raj was in Bluebirds one day before they figured out he could read just as good as Mrs. Martinez.

Raj and I saw each other a lot. Dad drinks a little. Uncle George drinks a lot. Dad and Uncle George sit on the porch, talk politics and drink beer. When they would get up to go get more, Mom forced them to take me along.

"We don't want no——."

"Take Harold. He needs to be around men who behave." Dad would grumble, but he knew that was her signal for him to slow down. She wanted to get Uncle George home without him getting into a fight downtown—or worse, tossed in jail again for bothering a drunk tourist.

"They are the ones that need supervision. Don't get back in the car if things get out of hand." Out of Hand= Phrases I Don't Understand= PIDU. I'm going to have a bunch of glossaries when I'm a famous crime novelist. The glossaries might even turn into a spy-code book that keeps the world safe for humanity.

Raj blinked a lot and didn't notice that his hair stuck straight up out of the back of his head. The other kids laughed because his pants were too short, and he had to hold them with his left hand to keep them from falling down. Raj was in the Green group even though his clothes didn't fit. His eyeglasses made him look like a frog or a grandpa or something. The teachers didn't care what we looked like. We just had to read their weird little booklets. Susan was pretty and always had a nice dress on. Susan was nervous and bit her lower lip. Raj stuck his tongue out to the left when he was concentrating. I told Susan to try sticking her tongue out when she read. Mrs. Martinez told me to be quiet and keep to my notebook.

13

One day my rocking kept me in for recess. I sat with the Red reading group. Gerald was stumbling over the word *under,* so I told him that he could skip it and figure it out from the picture or the rest of the sentence.

Mrs. Martinez frowned at me and started to tell Gerald he had to learn the word. She loved to do that. I tried to help Gerald. She didn't realize that was why he was frustrated. Adults try but they forget what it was like. I jumped up. "Mrs. Martinez we were Birdbirds last year. Nothing changed. Why are we Red now?"

"You need to learn the colors for art class so I changed the name."

"It's not working. Have you ever seen a red Bluebird? We still can't read." Gerald giggled. Mrs. Martinez told me to be quiet or I would miss another recess. The reading group during recess saved me from Devlin, so I just kept talking. Mrs. Martinez put me in the corner and let me rock in peace. Gerald whispered, "Thanks." before I left the group.

I was still in the Red group because they didn't test me until the end of my second year in first grade. My mom was too busy working to sign papers. She said busy but she really just didn't want to let them put me in retarded classes. It took so long they made me a library aid for part of the day. There was a kid with a helmet in the first grade for the third time that year. He moved to another school for retards. They called us special, but we knew what they meant. I looked it up. Special means something better, greater or otherwise different from what is the usual. We just got the "otherwise different" part of the dictionary. Teachers needed to have the kids call us a new name. That was the only reason. Kids already called us everything they could think of on the playground. I don't have to make a glossary of those words. Everyone knows those words. Loser, idiot, moron, retard, nose-picker. Now that I think about it, there are a few more words my mom won't let me say. MMWLMSTW4, MMWLMSTW5 and MMWLMSTW6 all have to do with body parts and things I'm not supposed to know. Maria brought a drawing her eighth grade brother drew of one of the words, but it didn't make much sense. Devlin almost beat her up for it. His goons said he'd get detention again which is kind of like Glacier Valley jail.

Dr. Williams finally got her report done. At least it got me out of first and second grade all in one shot. That's when I met Melvin. Devlin and Melvin were friends from the beginning of kindergarten. Their mothers liked to use the same park. Devlin and Melvin made the other kids scream while their moms gossiped in one of their cars, smoking cigarettes. Devlin was bad enough. Mr. Pimpleton didn't think I learned anything in math but I did. When you multiply the same thing it's more than just added. Together they were thugs squared. Extra bully with a side of fatso. Their moms just looked at magazine about movie stars and ignored the screams.

chapter 4

"They're going to let me keep my job here, Mrs. Greene."

"That's nice, Harold." Mrs. Greene was the only person besides my mother to call me Harold. I love Mrs. Greene almost as much as I do my mom. Mrs. Greene says she can't cook. I told her "I think my mom could teach you and then you could be my mom at school." She laughed when I told her that and gave me my stack of books to put away. Glacier Valley jumped me up to the third grade after the special tests. I'm not sure it matters much. They make us all march up and down the different grade hallways, but when a kid wears a helmets or rocks while he reads the hallways look all pretty much the same.

When I started first grade for the second time, there was a waiting list for the psychologist. Alaska is a big place. It took them a long time for me to take the test. Psychologist=Things My Mom Doesn't Want To Talk About=TMMDWTTA. It took my mom a long time to sign the papers. When Dad worked at Ketchikan Spruce, Mom could work part-time at night. She could take me to all of these different appointments. Ketchikan Spruce had good insurance, and so the doctors loved talking to Mom about how special I was and at such a young age. They even put me on another waiting list before I got to school. It made me kind of nervous. The only other person I ever heard that got put on a waiting list was a lady who needed a kidney. The lady got her kidney at the last second after the commercial for Buick. That was no surprise because people always come back to life after the commercial for Buick. Somebody is always trying to

16

kiss in the janitor's closet after the commercial for Skagway Streetcar Tours.

So ever since I was little, I wondered if I needed a kidney or my prostate checked. That's what the other commercials on TV talked about late on Saturday night between the ads for trucking school and the Franklin Mint selling silver dollar collections. When I was on the waiting list for the school psychologist, I tried to not be afraid that she was finding my kidney donor. Every time someone mentioned the psychologist, I would start rocking a little faster. When they told me that I was still on the waiting list I would rock a little slower. Susan was the only person to ever notice that I rocked different ways for different situations.

Mrs. Greene noticed I rocked, but she didn't seem to care. During story time, she gave me my own special book. She let me scoot way to the back. It was far away from the other kids and up against the edge of the couch she has near her desk. None of the kids talked during story time so I didn't rock as much. They switched my first grade teacher the second time to Mrs. Hanford. Teachers can only handle us for a year at a time. The kid with the helmet switches classes once or twice a year. His name is Harold too, but teachers don't mix us up the way they do when Jose Garcia and Jose Mencia end up in the same class. Mrs. Hanford was really nice and didn't yell at me as much to stop rocking. When she pronounced Harold, her voice sounded like wooden sticks slapping the concrete. It wasn't just my name. She said everybody's name like that. It made all of us sit up straight. Mrs. Hanford would come in at the end of story time and watch all of us for a couple of minutes. She was friends with Mrs. Greene. They would bring each other coffee in the office in the morning. They talked about their kids and trips to Cabo. It was like they live on another planet. They didn't think we were listening. I wondered what it's like to live like real rich kids. Some nights I would lay awake and wondered what would happen if my mom was the librarian and Mrs. Greene was my mom. I decided it would be a bad trade. Mrs. Greene can't cook. I would still wonder what it would be like to be a real rich kid who didn't rock and went to movies on the weekends with his friends.

I'm guessing it was because they were friends that Mrs. Hanford saw that I wasn't rocking as much. I looked happy with my special book. She asked Mrs. Greene if I could spend more than story time in the library. I was happy because it was quieter in the library. Pretty soon, I spent all day with Mrs. Greene and all the teachers whispered in the hall when I walked by. Principal Higgins and my mom didn't have clue. I guess the teachers thought it was okay because I was on a waiting list for a kidney.

The library was quiet like a hospital. The library didn't smell like a hospital. The day Grandma Frampton broke her hip and we were waiting, I didn't look like such a freak. This old guy was strapped to a chair and folded up like a pretzel. He smelled like bleach and diarrhea. Another lady was in a room groaning really loud. I rocked quite a bit. Dad kept hissing at me to stop. Grandma told him to be quiet so she could die in peace. She told Dad to bury her in Skagway. He said she was going to live until she was 100 and not talk that way. Uncle George didn't come to the hospital. He only comes around when he needs money between fishing jobs. He's been really close to a DUI a couple of times but Dad keeps taking him down to the VA to save him. Something about training and rehab.

So that second year in first grade turned out to be what saved me. Mrs. Greene was the first person to show me what books do. She was the first person to give me a notebook. She started by letting me just look at any of the books I wanted in the library. I'll tell you more about that later. I promised her to not destroy school property and that the smiling elephant was an accident. I was really gentle with the books and worked really hard at putting them back exactly where they were. I didn't want to get kicked out of the library. It was the only place that wasn't noisy. If another class was having story time I just went to my spot by the couch and took my special book and turned the pages.

One day my hands were really sweaty. I had to tell her a secret. I started to rock. I wanted to whisper but I just blurted. I said it too loud. "Mrs. Greene, I want to be a famous crime novelist like the ones on TV."

"Oh, you do? You want to be a writer?" I put my hands by my side. She didn't notice my palms.

"No, a novelist. A writer is too general." She smiled.

"Well, let me see how we can work that out for you, Harold."

"You can call me Rocky. All my friends call me Rocky."

"Harold—." Her voice flew away like sad birds. I started to rock a little, and she reached out and patted my shoulder. I let her touch me. Nobody else except Mom was allowed to touch me. It was hard to hear her because the palm of her hand was screaming at my body to jump. Screaming really loud in fact. I worked on it so the scream didn't go to my mouth. When I was little, the scream went straight to my mouth and then my mom's ears. Principal Wiggins had to give everyone a paper telling them not to touch me. It was an official school paper.

"All novelists write in journals or notebooks. I'll see what I can find." She lifted her hand to turn and look for something, and I could hear again. There it was. Shiny, blue and spiral. It was a big kid's notebook. My eyes got wide.

"Do you think I could have a small desk in here and have "Rocky" printed at the top here? Just like my first day of school?" I whispered it. "This is the nicest thing anybody has done for me, Mrs. Greene." Mrs. Greene turned away for a minute, and the sad birds flew away with her voice again.

"You're name is Harold. I need to call you by your name. We'll work something out." Her voice was low. She dabbed her eye and went to blow her nose.

I looked at the ground. Lord Dwark was choking my throat, but I couldn't stop the tears. Words blurted everywhere and I couldn't stop. "I need you to call me Rocky 'cause the kids call me Rocky, and we're not special we're just retarded and that's just another way to say otherwise different. Please, Mrs. Greene, please. If Rocky is on my desk, then the kids will know that I'm not just retarded. My desk is special. It's better. I need to count f-f-for something. Please print Rocky on the desk, I'll—." My thoughts were flying away. The bell rang for the next story time. I couldn't stop crying or talking. I was rocking really bad. Mrs. Greene hurried and got my special book. She took me by the hand and set me behind her desk in the glass office.

"It's okay, Har—, Rocky. Wait here." She closed the door behind her and did story time for the other kids. I finally laid down and let the linoleum cool my face. My cheeks were red. I snorted sobs for a while. I fell asleep.

"Rocky, Harold,—Rocky." The floor print was on my cheek. Drool came out. Mrs. Greene handed me my shiny blue notebook. It had ROCKY printed in pretty teacher writing. I sniffed.

"You can keep the notebook here, and I don't have to worry about the kids taking it. You can start writing like a famous crime novelist. I'll print a sign for your desk."

"Can I come in here again? I'll be good."

"I'll check with Mrs. Hanford and see what we can do." The sad birds left her voice and I handed her back the notebook. It was after lunch and the next class was coming in. I kept my head down. I went back to my spot by the couch and picked up my special book. My eyes dripped on the page, but I felt happy to feel the texture of the pages against my fingers, repeating over and over. It's soothing. Nobody understands that but Mrs. Greene and my mom.

Chapter 5

" —because before there were people like you who wanted to be famous crime novelists, people told stories to remember."

"I remember the important things."

"Yes you do, Rocky."

"Why do you remember that story?"

"Because Frank Reid is my great-great-grandfather. I've heard that story since I was your age."

"But aren't you supposed to just tell us stories out of the books?"

Mrs. Greene smiled. "I suppose so, Rocky. Why don't you write it down next time?"

"I can't keep my thoughts from running away, and you tell it with all those gestures."

"Well, why don't you try your best. If you think you miss something, come interview me to clean up the details. That's what real famous crime novelists do."

"Really?" Mrs. Greene patted me on the head and turned to greet the next class. They rumbled like the herd of cows that Mr. MacGregor lost on Main Street the year the cattle gates broke at the feed lot. People honked at the cows. The cows didn't care. The kids didn't care either. I hurried to my spot. Mrs. Greene told this story all day the year before when it was my first year in first grade, but I only heard it once. This year I was going to hear it over and over. I was going to write it down so she didn't get in trouble with the principal for telling us stories that weren't in the books. I've heard other adults

21

tell stories about Frank Reid. I think Mrs. Greene fudged so the kids would listen. That's okay. It's nice when people care if we listen.

FRANK REID SAVES SKAGWAY
By
Harold Reginald Blackbear Jones III, the famous crime novelist.
(with help from Mrs. Greene)

"Well, back in the 1800's, there was nothing here but this hill and dreams of gold in the Yukon." Mrs. Greene always started almost in a whisper to get the kids to listen.

"Some of us didn't quite make the gold rush. Sometimes it was because our wagons broke down. Sometimes it was because we had sick children. Sometimes it was because some no-good, dirty-rotten nose-pickers were just standing around Denver and decided to come stir up trouble in a new little town.

That's what Soapy Smith was. He was a no-good, dirty-rotten nose-picker just standing around Denver. He told all sorts of lies and told all sorts of stories to poor innocent dreamers trying their best to get to the gold rush. Even though the town was booming with people buying supplies, I have to tell you, there were quite a few scalawags and scoundrels!"

"What's a scalawag?" whispered Susan.

"Shh!" whispered all the other kids. I don't know how famous crime novelists keep up when someone is telling a story. I'll have to ask Mrs. Greene later.

"If you were part scoundrel and part scalawag you were worse than all the rest. That was Soapy. Being the worst made Soapy the boss of all the scalawags in town. Now I mean to tell you, all the people who were decent law-abiding citizens in Skagway were afraid for their lives. Soapy Smith would send his meanies and armpit-scratching bullies around town to take all the home baked apple pies back to Soapy. Even at Christmas time! It made all the children cry when they couldn't eat their Mommies' legendary apple pies that always won blue ribbons at the fair back in Loveland, Colorado.

It was so bad that all the children had to stay inside, so they wouldn't get trampled by horses and carriages Soapy was stealing from the docks. Everyone knew he was stealing the supplies and raising all the prices in the stores. Everyone was afraid of Soapy. So the people just stayed inside until all the stinky men were asleep. The shopkeeper would open the store for just a couple of hours and let them shop.

The problem was nobody was finding any gold. Nobody had much money. They couldn't pay Soapy's prices. He didn't care. He let the fruit rot in the boxes. He let the weevils eat the cereal. The town had a sheriff, but after one disappeared and the other left town to live with his sister in St. Louis, the position stayed vacant. Nobody who dared cross Soapy Smith would live to tell the tale. That's when Frank Reid arrived on the scene." Mrs. Greene smiled a little.

"Is that the statue over on Main Street?" Joe asked.

"Shhh!"

"Is that his real name? That's a strange name."

"Shhh!"

You see Frank was as brave as a lion and kind as a dove. When he saw that the children couldn't even go out to play, he decided to help a secret group of townspeople who were trying to figure out how to catch Soapy Smith and get him out of Skagway. Frank came as a land surveyor and had helped plot where they put all the buildings when Skagway was just starting out. Well the townspeople told him that standing up to Soapy was a terrible idea. They told him that he would be dead by morning if he didn't quit spouting all that talk about Soapy being a bully. They knew Soapy lied and cheated and always seemed to skirt out of town right before he got caught. When he got to Skagway he decided that he was just going to set up shop. Instead of looking like a bad guy, he dressed up really nice and acted like he was the mayor. The townspeople knew better, but nobody could stop him on account of him having all the crooks in town on his side.

"Well, living in fear all the time just ain't living. Not right." Frank Reid wasn't afraid. Since he was the surveyor, he went about inspecting the different businesses around town, pretending he was setting up a new building project. He was really trying to spy on Soapy. To his surprise, it was worse than he thought. Soapy Smith stole the manifest and wagon train schedules for the next three loads leaving Skagway. Whenever the gold came out of the hills, the big bankers in Seattle and San Francisco tried to make sure nobody would try to steal the gold. The bankers would put a reward out for almost double the price of the gold so thieves would do just what Soapy was planning. Turns out they never paid any reward. Once they got the gold back they locked up the poor sucker who turned it in. Soapy planned on robbing the wagon trains and then turning in the gold for the reward money. Maybe it would have been better for Skagway if Frank had just let him get away with it.

Frank Reid had seen enough. He took his rifle and stomped straight into the lair of Soapy Smith at the Buckshot Tavern. "Soapy Smith, you are under arrest!" Frank wasn't really sheriff. He was just trying acting like it to stop Soapy. Soapy didn't move a muscle. His smelly sidekicks just laughed and drew their guns on Frank. Soapy raised his hand real slow and lazy to keep them from filling him full of holes."

Then Mrs. Greene's voice got real gruff and mean-like. "Tell me, *sheriff*. What makes you think you won't disappear like the other men that tried to fill your shoes? You know I own this town." One of the sidekicks pulled back the hammer of his pistol with a 'click.' The other smelly scalawags all giggled. Frank straightened up to show he wasn't afraid, even though his heart was pounding inside his chest.

"Soapy, you can't push people around forever. I'll leave for the moment, but mark my words, Soapy. Skagway won't stand for your nonsense. I'm going to make sure of that." With that the thugs laughed and laughed. One even laughed so hard he shot the ceiling by accident and the plaster fell on Soapy's head.

"I said stop!" Soapy yelled at his crooks, standing up to dust himself off. "Get out, sheriff, before you end up like that ceiling up there. All broke to pieces! Everybody in town knows things don't go well when people cross me! With that Frank left. He wasn't done quite yet. He headed for the top of the hill.

"What was on top of the hill?" a little kid with broken glasses asked.

"Oh, that's just it." Mrs. Greene whispered. "There was one of the biggest spruce trees ever to see the light of day on top of that hill. Frank hiked the hills day after day thinking of how to catch Soapy. Knowing that Soapy would be looking for him, Frank climbed up in the spruce tree and watched everything going on in the town. He had a special spy glass he bought back in San Francisco when he thought about being a sailor. It was perfect for watching Soapy. He could even see the smile on Soapy's face the next morning as he sauntered out of the tavern." (Mrs. Greene did this little waddling step. I guess that meant she was sauntering.) Soapy sauntered because he thought Frank skedaddled out of town. The frowns on some of the towns-people made it seem like they believed the same thing." Mrs. Greene frowned and waved her hands like a magician.

Frank was sad but he knew it had to be that way for Soapy to let his guard down. Frank knew that nobody did everything perfect. He just had to find the weakness in Soapy's plan and then arrest him at the right moment. He hoped pretending to be sheriff would work. Sure enough it appeared Soapy had this one thug by the train station that was always falling asleep or smiling at the pretty ladies. He didn't pay much attention at all to what was happening on the loading dock.

Frank hatched a plan. He sneaked back into town and whis-pered the scheme to two or three of the strongest guys he could trust. They were all meeting in secret because Soapy gave his thugs commands to shoot anybody they found on the street after dark on sight. The secret group agreed. So the day the gold was scheduled to arrive, Soapy showed up in fine clothes with an empty wagon and a thug on each arm. They were going to rob the wagons in broad daylight. They knew nobody in town was going to challenge them. They loaded all the strong boxes into the wagon and then told the conductor to head on down the line. Soapy was beside himself with glee. He went to the tavern to celebrate with his thugs and they drank way too much chocolate milk, way until the evening."

"She means they got really drunk," Susan whispered.

"Shh!!"

But even with all that chocolate milk, he still worried about Frank Reid and those secret meetings. His thugs were passed out in the tavern so Soapy stumbled out to the wagons. When he found the first wagon, he clumsily pried open the wooden box and looked inside. Instead of gleaming gold bars, all he saw were common everyday bricks. It turned out that Frank and the other men made a deal with the transport wagons. They offloaded the gold at Dead Dog Gulch about 25 miles north of Skagway. Frank was going to end it once and for all, but he needed to make sure the gold and the townspeople were all safe. (The townspeople hid behind their shop windows while the secret meeting took place down near the docks.) Soapy Smith suspected it but now that his gold was gone he was livid. He didn't even wait for his thugs. He just huffed and puffed his way down to the dock and looked for the busiest building.

Frank was put on guard that night in case any of Soapy's thugs were out, but he didn't expect what he saw stumbling down toward him at the dock. There was Soapy himself waving a gun and making no sense. When their eyes locked. Frank drew his gun and got off a shot—but not before Soapy got off another shot. Frank's shot killed Soapy dead. The entire town rushed around Frank, cheering and planning a hero's parade. It just wasn't to be. Soapy's shot nicked Frank just enough that he had to lay in bed to try and get better. He didn't get better and died a few days later. Everyone was so sad. The town loved Frank so much they named the next city hall after him

"Where's that?" Gwen asked.

"We're not quite sure. There were bunches of forest fires. As soon as they got one building rebuilt another burned down. Most of the neighboring town of Dyea ended up moving into Skagway when the downtown burned to the ground. They're pretty sure that Main Street is in the right place. Folks ended up saying the ghost of Frank Reid still guards Skagway. That's why nobody like Soapy has been able to snuff it out forever like happened to Dyea.

"There's no such thing as ghosts." Gwen blurted.

"Are you sure?" Mrs. Greene said.

"There's no such thing as ghosts," Henry declared. Mrs. Greene smiled.

"That's what I used to say, Henry. That's what I used to say."

chapter 6

Every day after school in the third grade I ran like Derrick's drug dealer does from the cops. There wasn't tons of crime in Juneau. I watched Derrick to get material for my famous crime novels. The only difference was that Derrick's drug dealer was great at hopping that cyclone off in the alley off of 5th. It was six feet high. I was three feet high. I was running from Gigantor Melvin and Delvin. Teachers whispered that Melvin was at grade level but Dr. Williams had to qualify him for his behavior. Words For Notebook Friends=WFNF1 (Qualify sure is a strange word. Sometimes a word seems like it means the same thing when it doesn't. If your my friend then re-read the sentence. If you come across them later just re-read the sentence. Nobody is looking inside your head. That's impossible.) Mom gets tons of letters saying she qualifies for a Visa card. Tourists use lots of Visa cards. I never understood why we qualified. When they stuck you as a Bluebird they didn't give you a Visa card to spend down at those t-shirt shops on the dock. Mr. MacKay didn't care what Melvin was qualified for. He just wrote him up every day and sent him to the office. They switched Melvin to Mrs. Homer's class.

Melvin was the reason why I had Mrs. Greene hold my notebooks. I ate everything at school lunch. Mom made me take the backpack. She said to put homework in it but I took it to school and jammed it full of the worksheets— just to fit in with the other kids. All of us had a back pack. Some kids had lunches their mothers gave them. A few of the kids took the papers home and brought them back to get their gold stars. My backpack looked like a hair clog Dad pulled out of the drain. I had papers, banana peels—you name it, it was in there. Melvin loved to catch me and swing me around by my backpack, sit on my chest and thump his middle finger knuckle on my WFNF2 (In case you are my friend the word is sternum. It's a bone right in the middle of your chest that protects your heart. If the word doesn't make sense, just skip it and see if the next sentence helps you figure it out.)

We would all go down to Mr. Pizinski's PE class after lunch. This helped Mr. Clausen, our third grade teacher. He was old and said he was just about ready to be tired. It was true. He couldn't get his beer belly off his desk by the end of the day. In gym we would play dodge ball most days. Mr. Pizinski made me play. The other Harold with the helmet was left along the side lines to drool. My teachers had a conference with my mom after Dr. William's report that made them push me into doing more things. That mostly meant that Mr. Pizinski pushed me into being Melvin's target.

I was just lucky that Deprecia was there. She lived three doors down from me. Principal Higgins was nowhere near the size of a house but I was never quite sure about Deprecia's dad, Mr. Bane. Mr. Bane played college football and worked as a security guard at McDonald's in the morning so that none of the teenagers would upset the tourists. Mr. Bane was happy to tell you that his family fought in the Spanish American War. They lived all the way from Dyea to Juneau for 100 years. That's what Deprecia said anyway. I never argued. I didn't know if she was going to try out for the foot-ball team at the college but Mr. Bane had something called a full ride scholarship. It must have been what he bought the Toyota pick-up with last year. He was a local hero on our street. He went to college instead of working a fishing boat. He'd been on television during a bowl game.

Deprecia was dark as midnight and talked like a fog horn no matter how many times the teacher said to use an inside voice. When she was around she would stick up for me. The first Dodge ball game Melvin flattened me. She got mad and yelled, "Pick on somebody your own size!" She beaned Melvin with a fast ball to the groin. Mr. Pizinski blew his whistle. Deprecia had to come out because of the foul. Both of them came out of the game. Melvin had tears in his eyes and couldn't stand up straight. I whispered "Thanks" when we lined up to go back to the room.

When we got back Mr. Clausen was still sitting there tired. He looked up at the clock. Every day after PE we had ten minutes before the bell to go home. It meant I had ten minutes to figure out how I was going to avoid Melvin and Delvin. If they beat me, I couldn't tell Mom. She worked at night full time by the time I was in the third grade. I tried to not stress her out too much. All of the bills and waiting lists piled up. Things got a little better when we moved to Skagway later. But not much.

Mr. Clausen would have us all line up in his room when we came back from PE or recess. He leaned on the desk when he stood like it was propping him up. He barked and mumbled at us to get our backpacks, stack our chairs and stand behind our desks. Then he had this contest that I always lost. It was a teacher trick that worked great to make us quiet. I always lost the contest. In a royal tone of voice, he would announce the name of each kid dismissed to the bus. The rules to the game were easy. The person who stayed like a silent statue left first. I knew I was going to lose every time. Trying to be normal for those 90 seconds stressed me out. I would start to rock. I was always last. Melvin didn't care for the rules He would make a fake fart noise or fart for real. The real contest was for the other kids not to giggle at Melvin or Devlin. I tried to explain why I lost the game to Mr. Clausen once but he told me, "Rules are rules. You'll understand when you're older." He mumbled about a teacher's betiredment and the market.

Mr. Clausen's game turned into a final count down for a track race of retards. He would always hold us one minute after class as our final punishment. He might as well been the track judge with the gun raised. Natalie ran track. I went once but the gun made me scream. Mom had to take me home. I was closest to Mr. Clausen's desk. If we ran when he let us go he kept us another minute. We had to do that "I'm not running" waddle little kids always do around a swimming pool until we got to the front door of the school. Most of the time Melvin hip checked me into the door to get a head start.

Some days I would risk it and break into a run in the last five feet in front of the door. If I got enough of a head start then they would give up because they were both pretty pudgy. They had to catch me in the first block or two. I got hit by a car once running a red light to escape Melvin. The car used a bunch of MMWLMSTW in Russian, screeched to a halt, and hit me with his bumper. I didn't care. Devlin and Melvin counted on the lights catching me, so they could make a grab and pummel me behind O'Malley's Fish Bar where Devlin's mom worked. Devlin wiggled his belly in school. Devlin said he started a beer belly early. He ate all the fish and chips he wanted.

Then one day an angel decided I wasn't supposed to be beat up any more. Running my butt off, I saw something out of the corner of my eye. Just off to the left was Naches Avenue. The houses there were built in Juneau right around 1900. That's where the rich people lived. The green one a couple blocks from the school was abandoned and boarded up after a fire. Even Derrick was scared of it. I'm positive it had more than vampires and dragons in there after dark. But right by the fire hydrant there was this giant tree. I noticed it that day. I still had to run my usual route. The traffic lights were with me. Melvin and Devlin got stuck behind the flashing red hand.

All that night I ran the new route in my head. Making that turn had to work or I'd be toast. We lost Mr. Clausen's game just like every day except I took a risk and bolted right outside the door from Mr. Clausen's room. He yelled at me to come back, but I ignored him. He kept yelling until Devlin and Melvin stopped. They would pound me later for getting them into trouble. I figured that it evened out since they had already been pounding me. Seemed to make sense.

I slid right behind Dulce and tucked myself low where I could watch the street. I named the tree Dulce because she let me stay as long as I wanted. She let me rock all I wanted. Maybe it was already her name because somebody carved "Dulce loves John" into the trunk.

I waited until it was almost dark that first day. Mom kind of freaked out which made Dad freak out. When Dad freaked out, I rocked worse. He didn't understand the rocking. He always thought I was broken, and he was fixing me. I wasn't broken. He wasn't fixing me. That's what he said every time. It's what fixed him when he was my age. I believed him and prayed every night that the fix would take. I'd wake up and be Harold Reginald Blackbear Jones the III instead of Rocky. I was lucky Mom made his favorite dinner and had plenty of his favorite beer. I got there before he got that headache that always made it worse. He wasn't fixing me, but he tried.

Chapter 7

Mrs. Greene didn't just help me finish writing the story in the notebook. If you want to know the truth, Mrs. Greene solved an even bigger problem in my life. She figured out how to get the words from stop hopping all over the page like frogs after a spring rainstorm. The teachers kept this big secret about letting me spend most of the day with Mrs. Greene my second year in the first grade.

I loved the feel of the pages on my fingers. I could flip through the big book in about three hours if nobody bothered me. Most days somebody bothered me, and Mrs. Greene had to teach me how to ignore them. It didn't always work. Anytime I saw the shadow of someone walking by or all the noise of the kids coming into the room, I started to rock. If they kicked my foot, I barked a scream. They would giggle. Mrs. Greene would try to steer them away. Most of the time I like to rock backward and forward, but in a pinch I can rock side to side.

Other people rock. Mrs. Brothers, the music teacher, always rocks back and forth when there is music playing. All the moms with baggie eyes and little babies rock from side to side. Nobody tells them anything. My mom had to come down to this big meeting one day during my second year in first grade. They wanted Dad to come too, but he couldn't get the time off. His bosses always yelled at him about making mistakes when he left his desk. He wanted to be there all the time to make sure they couldn't yell at him. I was glad when they didn't yell at him. That meant he didn't feel like he needed to fix me as much.

I noticed that teachers did the same thing when they had problems with Principal Wiggins. She started to scrunch that one eyebrow like a raven getting ready to fly away again, and the teachers came back into the classroom upset. When they came in too upset, they acted like Dad, only they didn't have a chance to drink any beer. I'm sure that when they got home, some of them had a chance to drink beer. They fixed their real rich kids the same way my dad tried to fix me.

I mean it's not like my dad is like Emily Flennigan's dad. They lived in the house just behind ours. He's not trying to fix anything. He just drinks, cusses and breaks stuff. Once and a while Emily comes over for dinner. We all act very polite and nice. Even Dad. We don't ask any questions, and my parents discuss the weather. It is all very formal like we've seen in the movies when the queen and the duke are sipping tea in a big room with a fireplace. They have rooms as big as three of our houses complete with huge paintings and silk curtains. Queens and dukes have a butler. We don't.

At the big meeting we had I kept wondering if Emily was ever going to have her meeting. I doubted it. Emily was a Robin. On top of that, she was one of the quietest girls in the class. All the teachers loved her if they ever remembered her name. She was great at never raising her hand. She just bit her lower lip and made sure her answers looked mostly like Lupe's and Brian's. Lupe and Brian sat in the front row. They passed out the nice pencils or the hall passes. They were both Eagles, but you didn't have to have me tell you that. All the teachers smiled when Lupe or Brian answered the questions.

I started rocking right away when the meeting started. My mom had given me all my meds. They said that I couldn't take my special book into the room. Mrs. Greene sat next to me on the other side from my mom. My mom tried to pat me on the shoulder for good luck. She knew that her fingers were screaming in my brain that someone was touching me. She knew that if this meeting didn't go right in front of all the teachers, I wouldn't be able to go to the real school. Mrs. Greene knew the same thing. None of us said it. We were all dreading what the doctors and other teachers were going to say about me being a Bluebird for the three years in a row.

Mrs. Greene said not to worry and that she had a secret plan, just like Frank did back in 1898 with Soapy Smith when he wanted to rob the wagons. "You're not going to shoot Mr. Clausen are you?" I whispered before it all started. There was a fat man with thick glasses, a wrinkled suit, and a yellow tie covered in school busses. His frown almost reached his lapels. He reminded me of Deprecia's Bassett hound. The one Mr. Bane kept in the back yard as a guard dog.

Mrs. Greene smiled. "Well, I hope not, but let's see what bug-eyed Mr. Jacobs says. Just remember what we've been practicing." I took deep breathes and tried to slow down the rocking. Eventually I gave up and just tried to pretend I was a post stuck in the ground. I let my mind wander. I pretended a dove landed on my head. I didn't want it to land. Lord Dwark walked over to me and stood guard. My heart quit pounding as fast.

"Harold? Harold?" Mr. Jacobs was calling my name. Mom and Mrs. Greene let my mind wander. Mr. Jacobs didn't. I started to rock and look down at the table after blinking a couple of times. "Harold, do you agree that you need more help?" I blinked.

The adults around the table all talked before he talked to me. Just because I was concentrating on being a post with a dove on my head, didn't mean I hadn't heard anything they were saying. They went around the whole table. Some of them were teachers. Some of them had big words for titles. All of them with big words for titles had glasses and grey hair. Except Mrs. Balm. She dyed her hair really black. She pretended to be a Tlingit on the weekends for the tourists. She got in trouble for trying to pass off bad beads one year. Dad sais that she's a menace. Dad said she made three times the amount of money off the tourists as the tribe. Dad hated the hippies like her for being Tonto and Bozo the clown all wrapped into one. I don't know who Tonto is. I don't know who Bozo is. She gave me a sweet smile. I knew those smiles were dangerous. She was one of the white ladies who called herself Moonflower. She wore strange flower dresses. She smelled like vanilla bean lotion.

"I know how to read," I whispered.

Mr. Clausen scooted his chair. "Now, Harold I'm sure you think you can—."

"Jerry, why don't you just let him continue?" Mrs. Greene didn't like Mr. Clausen. He called the meeting to get back at me for running out of his room. I told Principal Wiggins about losing the game all the time.

"Well I just don't want him to get his—."

"I'm sure we can all rest assured that the entire staff has Harold's best interest in mind." Mr. Jacobs took his glasses off and pinched the bridge of his nose. When he could see again, he asked me to repeat what I said. He was looking at Mr. Clausen to tell him to be quiet. Mr. Clausen's nose got red, but he didn't say anything.

"I can read."

"Are you sure you just don't think you can read?" Mrs. Balm smiled. They started to argue again, so I finally just ignored them and looked over at the sheet Mrs. Greene had in front of her and started at the top. "Case Manager: Phyllis Balm."

These are all in capitals so I yelled them. "PLEASE REMEMBER THAT THIS INFORMATION IS CON—FI—." They were big words. I started to rock. I was concentrating. I looked up at Mrs. Greene who was smiling at me. She nodded at me to continue. "CONFIDENTIAL! These aren't in capitals so I'll stop yelling, Mr. Jacobs. I can't stop rocking but I can keep reading if all of you be quiet." They were all quiet while I read. "This sheet needs to be kept in a confidential, locked lo—cation. If you don't have a locked place to keep this page, or if you have the information and don't care to keep it, please review this page and then shred it. I am sending this out again as a reminder, and because many students' IEP's have been updated since I sent this out last time.—."

"This is a set up. You made him memorize that. He can't—." Mr. Clausen's cheeks were red. You could see little purple lines on his face. "Even if he did read it, he doesn't understand it!"

"Honestly!" Mrs. Greene was standing up now. Mr. Jacobs took his glasses off again and waved them at Mrs. Greene to have her sit down.

"He never reads in my class."

"You never have anybody read in your class!"

"I've been teaching for 30 years and—."

"Teachers, please." Mr. Jacobs frown went a little lower as he looked over his glasses at both Mrs. Greene and Mr. Clausen. Mrs. Balm was drawing circles on her pad. "It appears we have a minor miracle on our hands, and it would be nice to gain some insight into how Harold here made such rapid progress."

"I learned to read with Legos."

Dr. Williams finally spoke up. "Harold is a special case of ASD. It appears that he has close to an eidetic memory when it comes to words. I might tend to agree with Mr. Clausen. I'm not sure Harold really understands what he just read."

"Tell them what you told me, Harold." Mrs. Greene said.

"Words are like a flock of birds that get scared in my head. They might be all sitting on the page just minding their own business. Then kids start talking or pulling on my backpack and the birds all fly away."

"What else did you tell me?"

"When I visited Grandma Frampton in Skagway, I realized that your brains go slower than molasses. For all of you, the words are like the cars on the White Pass Yukon train. Your brains must be weighted down like the train. All the words are hooked together."

"When I tested Harold, he could spell words that put him as a sophomore in college. He just had no way to put the words in context."

"Why didn't you ever read in Mr. Clausen's class, even after you moved out of first grade?"

"He never asked me to. He said rules are rules and something about betiredment." Mr. Clausen's cheeks got red again.

"Of course I asked him to read. I've been teaching for 30 years. Kids are different today. I asked him to read every day!"

"You asked Emily to read every day. You took away my special book and said I couldn't have it back until I read the sentence." Mrs. Greene was starting to get purple. I put my hand on her hand even though it meant my hand was on fire and screaming at me to stop touching. They never understand the noise it makes in my head. I started rocking and groaning.

"I'm not sure he's going to be able to complete this meeting," Mom said next.

"Mr. Clausen, please refrain from further interruption." Mr. Jacobs said. "Can you let us know when it is too much, Harold?" I nodded. "Can you tell us how the Legos helped?"

"Mrs. Greene did some experiments. Not like I'm a lab rat experiment. My dad says he doesn't want any of you doing lab rat experiments and sucking my brain out with electric helmets.

"Harold—." Mom patted me on the knee three times to signal me to focus.

I paused with all of them and then saw Mrs. Greene out of the corner of my eye. I kept going. "The first experiment was with the notebook. I told Mrs. Greene I couldn't write. She gave me big kid books without pictures. She told me I was a big kid. She told me that it used to be somebody's job all day to copy important words from one book into another. It was slow at first, but she said I was doing great. I copied and copied and copied. That's why I needed so many notebooks."

"Did that help?" Dr. Williams asked.

"At first it was like flipping the pages of my favorite book. I just liked understanding that I could do the same thing over and over and wouldn't get yelled at. She even called me important."

"What other—experiments, did Mrs. Greene do that you liked?" Mr. Jacobs cleared his throat when he talked.

"She gave me a marker with some Legos. I told her that all of your rules swim around like fish and that I would put the rules in a zoo where I could be the zookeeper. She let me build a zoo in the back. Then later on she told me that the word "the" was a friend. She let me set up the Legos and told me to build a zoo. One day she gave me a book, and told me I was the zookeeper. It was an easy book but I finally understood why your brains are so slow. Then it was my chance to try and experiment. I copied the easy book into my notebook. She said that the word "the" was the door to the cage and that the other words were the animals. She said I could change cages and animals around if I opened the door. I tried it. That's why I am going to be a famous crime novelist now. Now I can write my own words for your molasses brains." Mr. Jacobs chuckled. Mom patted me on my knee three times.

"But Son, why didn't you ever read in Mr. Clausen's class if you could for Mrs. Greene?"

"Mr. Clausen's class was always too noisy. The words just flew away. Sometimes they even turned into bees and buzzed so loud I could barely hear what he was saying from the board at the front of the room."

"On that paper you just read, Harold. What did it mean?"

"Confidential means private. So this is supposed to be private. Mr. Clausen isn't supposed to talk on the phone about us. The rest of the words flew away when all of you started yelling."

"Dr. Williams, please make a note in the minutes reminding me to have a word with Mr. Clausen about protocols."

"Can I please still be a library aide?" I asked.

"Do you think you will be able to read in Mr. Clausen's class?"

"I doubt it. I want to, but the words fly away. Melvin chases me. Dodgeball hurts."

"We'll see what we can do." Mr. Jacobs tapped his pad of paper three times. Mrs. Greene hugged my shoulder. Even though my shoulder yelled bloody murder for her to stop, the scream didn't come out of my mouth. She stayed back and talked to Mom some more after everyone left. Mr. Clausen glared at me. I needed the word betiredment=PIDU2. I kept rocking until everyone was gone. I asked Mrs. Greene if I could interview her later about the meeting for my notebook. Mom brought me my favorite cough drop. It always took time for me to suck on that cough drop without chewing for me to calm down enough after a meeting. Mom kissed me on the forehead. Her lips don't make my forehead scream. Just strangers' lips.

"Why don't I make you some spaghetti, Harold?"

"That would be great, Mom."

Chapter 8

Dad was wrong. Grandma didn't live to be 100. He mumbled about it, but he figured out how to get her buried up in the Skagway cemetery. Not many people can do that anymore. He's just glad that the owner of the Skagway Streetcar Company is respectful. He says he doesn't want Grandma's bones to end up in a tourist shop somewhere. Mom said he was being silly.

Mom told me it wasn't my fault that we moved to Skagway after the funeral. She's lying. She thinks because I always talk too loud and rock that I don't understand. I don't have an inside voice—even when I whisper. I'm not sure what that even means. My hearing is fine. It's just the way I talk.

They had the funeral on a Tuesday. A mist came up off of Lynn Canal. I'm pretty sure it was coming to take her away. I looked for Frank Reid in the mist but didn't see anything. This is pretty much all seventh grade now. Thanks for reading my notebook. Thanks for being patient. There wasn't much to tell after the third grade. Mr. Clausen took an early betiredment. He wasn't in class for three days after our meeting. Principal Wiggins changed me back to Mrs. Hanford's class for the rest of the year. I didn't care. They let me stay with Mrs. Greene. I just stopped by Mrs. Hanford's for recess and lunch. I guess I was like Harold with the helmet. At least they didn't send me to retard school.

I spent most of my afternoons behind Dulce. Melvin and Devlin gave up chasing. The teacher who replaced Mr. Clausen didn't play the same game at the end of the day. She just assigned Melvin detention for farting. He had to clean the boards a lot. Devlin got fat eating all the time. He didn't want to run. I still hung out behind Dulce. I could tuck behind the tree and watch traffic go by. Dulce was my own secret fort where nobody but Lord Dwark could come. Sometimes I wrote in my notebook. I was practicing to be a famous crime novelist. Mrs. Greene calls it research.

Up here in Skagway there are tons of trees. They aren't wrapped up in a city. It's more like the trees wrap up Skagway. Dad says I have to be careful. They don't have a doctor in town. He told me not to break my arm. It's too small for a doctor. Dad likes it that way. I'm glad Melvin is not in Skagway. Once when Melvin caught me on the playground, my shirt ripped again. The teacher didn't believe me. I didn't tell her that dad tried to fix me once and a while. It was Melvin that time. The school had a meeting with just my mom. She was really sad. Grandma Frampton died later that year. Before I started the seventh grade, Dad moved us up here to live in her old house. His bosses at his last job were getting worse. He remembered hunting and fishing all the time. He moved us up here.

Mom wanted to keep her job. It was too far. The bills and waiting lists were piling up. Dad said not to worry. They could eat what was left in Grandma's cupboards until the big ships came. Dad said Skagway looked like a jelly doughnut on an anthill in the summer time. He was right. This place is crawling with tourists. Dad said it was just a matter of finding out which two or three jobs she wanted. Dad used to work on road crews and fishing boats. He's older now.

"Unbelievable!" That's what Mrs. Greene said when I walked in to tell her the news that we were leaving. She didn't say it to me. She wasn't facing me. She was on the phone with her Aunt Edna. Her Aunt Edna was the great-grand daughter of Frank Reid. Mrs. Greene was really upset. "They can't do that!" She chattered on and on like I do when my thoughts run away. She waved her hands at some invisible person. She pointed her finger. She was really upset. I hope she didn't break the phone when she hung it up. She still had her back to me. "Stupid MMWLMSTW7!" I couldn't believe it. Mrs. Greene spun around when I made a noise. "Oh, Rocky! I didn't—well, you won't—."

"Don't worry, Mrs. Greene. Dad says a lot worse." I tried to tell her I was leaving to Skagway but just started rocking and crying. She got the story out of me. She gave me my name card from the desk. I calmed down. "Mrs. Greene?"

"Yes, Rocky."

"Who was unbelievable?"

"Oh somebody with a bunch of shell companies. They want to move Skagway and build an ugly huge hotel on the canal for the tourists."

"People make that much money selling shells?" I asked. Mrs. Greene smiled.

"No, Honey. It's just that Skagway is where I'm from. My Aunt Edna still lives there. It would be a crime to put up a hotel and move the town."

"Well, if it's a crime, I'll investigate it for you when I get there."

"That would be nice, Honey. Don't worry. We'll see each other again. I come up during the summers. I might just have to come up more often to check on Aunt Edna." She smiled and messed with my hair.

"You could visit me too."

"I could visit you. In fact, wait a minute. Take this home to your mother." She scribbled on a piece of paper.

"What's this?"

"Aunt Edna's phone number at the Skagway Streetcar Tour Company. She's their secretary. Tell your mom to tell Aunt Edna that you know me. She'd love to hear from you."

"I will, Mrs. Greene."

There was the usual meeting with Skagway Middle School, but Mom smoothed everything out. She mentioned Mrs. Greene. That made it better. Mrs. Clements grew up with Mrs. Greene. They talked on the phone, and Mrs. Clements said Skagway was smaller. She said they would try to find me a quiet place. It was a good thing I knew how to read. The best part of not worrying about getting beat up by Melvin was that I had time to investigate the crime. It was a crime to build an ugly hotel. Mom told me not to bother people. Mrs. Clements assigned me to write a story for the school paper. She asked me to find out what people thought of the hotel. Most of the shopkeepers were happy to talk to me. Not Mr. Schumacher.

"Who put you up to this? Are you one of those rabble rousers?" Mr. Schumacher was mad. PIDU3=rabble rousers.

"No, sir. Mrs. Clements asked me to do a story on the hotel. People are telling me what they think." I started rocking.

"Well, what are they saying?" he spouted. I rocked more. He wasn't nice.

"Mrs. Graves loves you. She's so happy to get a new house in Dyea she has almost all of her things packed already. Mr. Henderson says you stole his papers with lot number 1070818981."

"What does Crazy Larry know anyway? He cuts out horoscopes every day and drinks orange soda like it's the last bottle. Even found him going down the street in his long johns and a tinfoil hat last year."

"Mrs. Cooper says she likes your shop. Mr. Cooper says your jerky tastes like crap. Mrs. Tyler said that the city council went along with it because you gave them money. She says the company that sells shells smells fishy. I told her everything in Skagway smelled fishy. That's why there were so many boats catching fish." I was going to say more about how Mr. Feeney thought it was a great way of keeping the tourists around, but Mr. Schumacher started to make fun of me. "Well, R-R-Rocky. Do you stutter too? Leave your nose out of other people's business!" He waved me out of the store and flipped the closed sign. Things were slow in October. Lots of shops were closed, so the men could go hunting.

He was the grumpiest about the company that sells shells. It was actually an international conglomerate. I asked Mom what that was. She said she didn't know, but it sounded big. Conglomerate is MMDUTW2 in this notebook. Mom's pretty smart. The man that started the company was Hendrick Vankersloot. Don't worry if you can't pronounce it. Just picture someone in a suit and tie with horns on this head. That's what I did.

I read more about him on the computer at school. He became famous for holding companies hostage at gunpoint or something. He would hold companies hostage and put together hostile takeovers. I would give up my company too if someone put a gun to my head. It doesn't seem fair. Mrs. Clements said that there weren't any guns involved. I asked her why he was holding companies. She didn't really know. She just said it made him rich enough to buy Skagway. She said that's why he can pay everyone a settlement and get the city council to go along with the plan. Mrs. Clements is not like Mrs. Greene. She's nice but she always looks tired.

"You need a headline for your story, Rocky. I need to finish the school paper."

"SKAGWAY TAKEN HOSTAGE!" I yelled. She frowned. Mrs. Greene would have laughed. I missed her.

"Rocky, please quiet down. We need something less threatening. We don't want to be one of those newspapers in the grocery line."

"The ones where aliens ate the brains of Elvis?"

"Yes. Those newspapers. We have a nice, respectable newspaper that does Skagway Middle School a service. How about SKAGWAY CONSIDERS NEW HOTEL COMPLEX?"

"I guess so."

"Then it's settled. Oh, and Rocky——."

"Yes, Mrs. Clements?"

"Try to avoid Mr. Schumacher. He's not a happy man and he's the mayor. I don't want any trouble for you."

"Can I go write in my notebook, now? I'm starting a story about the ghost of Frank Reid. Can we publish that one?"

"That would be fine."

Chapter 9

"There! Arrest him!"

"Now come on, Ralph. I'm not going to arrest him. We're just here to talk." Mrs. Clements brought me down to the office. She let me keep my notebook. I was rocking pretty bad. I was looking at the ground and not at Mr. Schumacher. This time Dad was there in the office with me. For once he wasn't trying to fix me. He wanted to fix Mr. Schumacher.

"You lay a finger on my boy Ralph, and I'll—."

"You'll what, Harry. Run to Juneau? Catch your quota of salmon?" Dad stood up. Dad clenched his fists. Sheriff Tate stepped in between. Principal Smith looked up. Principal Smith told everyone that he wasn't related to Soapy Smith. He told everyone that Smith was the most common name in the world. I wasn't sure it was that common in Mexico. Mom said we weren't in Mexico. She said to be quiet in the meeting.

"Gentlemen, why don't we just have a seat?" Mr. Schumacher didn't like the idea. Principal Smith waved him to the conference table.

"You need to arrest him. HVI is really mad." Mr. Schumacher was giving me the stinky eye. That's what Natalie called them. I didn't smell anything, but they were definitely stinky eyes.

"Slow down. Can you please just let us know what this is about?"

"Someone went to the construction site last night and pulled up all the surveyor stakes. They spray painted "Not my markers" on some of the plywood they had stacked there." Sheriff Tate said.

"Don't you have all of that locked up?" My dad asked.

"Yes, that's why you should arrest him. He's the rabble rouser that started the whole thing!"

"You fell on your head one too many times, logging Ralph," my dad laughed. I was rocking pretty bad. It was hard to focus.

Principal Smith looked at Mrs. Clements. "It appears Mr. Schumacher did not appreciate the stories Harold wrote in the school newspaper."

"It's a middle school newspaper! We only print a few copies and hand them out to the students. All he did was write a story about the hotel complex and a ghost story about Frank Reid." She said.

"He's a menace." Mr. Schumacher said.

"I'm going to pop you, Ralph." My dad was getting mad. He stopped laughing.

Sheriff Tate tried to keep them calm. "Janie, it's just that we're a pretty small town. What the kids bring home everybody reads."

"Did he write something that wasn't true?"

"That's not the point. He put the fool idea in somebody's head that they can stop this project." Mr. Schumacher said.

"I just wrote down what they told me," I said. I said it too loud. I was getting agitated, and there were bees buzzing in my head.

"That makes it even worse! To think people would go around believing this retard!" My dad jumped the table and punched Mr. Schumacher in the nose. It was a big scene. I hid under the table. Sheriff Tate pulled Dad off of Mr. Schumacher.

"That's assault! I know my rights! Arrest him! I know my rights!"

Sheriff Tate spun Dad around. "Geez, Harry this isn't high school anymore. You know I've got to do something now."

"I know my rights! Arrest him! Assault!" Mr. Schumacher ranted. His bloody nose was dripping on the carpet. The blood was going to be hard to get out of the carpet.

"Are you going to let him get away with that?" Mrs. Clements was standing up and waving at Mr. Smith as Sheriff Tate led Dad out of the office. Mr. Schumacher sat down and tilted his head back. He was trying to get the bleeding to stop.

"Please take Harold back to the room, Mrs. Clements. We'll discuss this later."

"But—."

"I need to speak with Mr. Schumacher in private, Mrs. Clements. Please take Harold back to the room." Mr. Smith was quiet but firm.

"Come on, Harold." I was rocking and agitated. I needed to get the bees to stop buzzing in my head. She didn't have a cough drop. She didn't understand. "Come on Harold. The grown-ups have to talk." I was rocking and rocking. She said it a couple more times but it wasn't helping. The bees were buzzing louder and louder.

"Oh, honestly!" Mr. Schumacher got up and reached under to drag me out from under the table. He didn't read the official school paper. He wasn't supposed to touch me. I couldn't stop the screaming on my arm when he grabbed me. The screaming left my mouth this time. I screamed and kicked and screamed and kicked. He wouldn't let go. All the bees were red now in my head, and I bit his hand.

"Ow! That stupid retard bit me! Arrest him! Assault!" He let go.

"MR. SCHUMACHER!" Principal Smith used to play football. He was taller than Mr. Schumacher. Mr. Schumacher sat down. I crawled back under the table, rocking and screaming. They all had to leave the room. It took time. I stopped screaming. It took more time. Mom came to the school. She hugged me. She waited. She gave me a cough drop. It took even more time. It was dark when we left the school. Principal Smith was the only one there. His tie was loose. Mr. Schumacher was gone.

"I'm sorry, Harold. We won't let him come back to school." Principal Smith said. "Mrs. Jones, we need to sort some things out. Is it okay if Harold comes back in a few days?"

Mom gave him stinky eyes. She didn't talk. She wanted to say MMWLMSTW1, MMWLMSTW2 and definitely MMWLMSTW4. She didn't talk. Skagway isn't that big. We walked home. She made me spaghetti. She even let me use the earmuffs to cut down the noises. I used them when I was little. She made the house quiet as possible. It was pretty easy to have a quiet house with Dad not there. Natalie wanted to whine about not watching TV. She didn't. She came and told me she was sorry about the mean man. She kissed my forehead. Mom and Natalie don't make my skin scream.

I fell asleep. When I woke up, Mom made pancakes. I left the earmuffs on all morning and wrote in my notebooks. Mrs. Greene let me take my special book when we moved. I turned the pages from start to finish three times. Mom left me alone for most of the day. I hope Daphne didn't know about what happened. This was before she threw Shakespeare at me. This was right at the beginning of the school year. Daphne knew. Skagway isn't that big.

Chapter 10

Mr. Schumacher didn't know it. He declared war on the Tlingits. That's what Dad said when he got out of jail. I'm not sure that was a good idea. Not a real war like you read about with the Apaches or the Cherokees down in the other states. Tlingits always try to help people out. Alaska is a hard place to live, and if we don't help each other, everybody freezes and dies. Mr. Schumacher was the mayor, and he gave my dad something to fight for when he had Dad arrested.

I went back to school after a couple of days. The tribal lawyer came up the next weekend and reviewed the case. Mrs. Clements helped me write the story about Mr. Schumacher and my dad. She helped like Mrs. Greene did. She put other words in there when I messed up. She asked if she could borrow a notebook that I finished. I shook my head "No." Then she asked if she could type some of it out if I watched her. That was okay. Ever since Melvin pounded on me I didn't trust anyone. Only Mrs. Greene could hold my notebooks. Mrs. Clements gave what she typed to my mom. My mom told her thank you and took it down to the jail when the lawyer got there.

Dad came home with a big smile on his face. He had to spend a week in jail so the ferry could get the lawyer here. He didn't care. He said that Mr. Schumacher was lucky he wasn't sued for what he did to me. Dad said what Mrs. Clements typed helped. I didn't understand. Mr. Schumacher just didn't read the official school papers. Every school I went to put official school papers in my IEP that told

48

people they couldn't touch me without my permission. It's like some autistic law or something. That wasn't the only thing. The lawyer also told Dad that the tribe had already had a run in with Mr. Schumacher.

"Schumacher tried to help HVI add gambling to their monster hotel. They ended up having to cut that part of the project because of tribal red tape. I'm going to make sure they have even more red tape when it comes to this project. They can't just toss money around and kick us out of our own town."

"We could use the money, Harry." Mom glanced at her pile of bills. "There's nothing wrong with a business making money. That's what they do." It got quiet.

"Now you're talking like Schumacher." Dad was irritated.

"I just mean I can't find a job. Skagway is small."

"It will work out. We're strong here in Skagway. We've always made it work."

"But the plans for the new houses they want to build over the Dyea site look pretty."

"We've lived here since Skookum Jim helped them cut the paths."

"It's not the same. It's not 1890. A nice house would be nice." Mom said.

"We're all going down to the next city council meeting. Schumacher isn't going to get away with this."

"Harry—."

"Schumacher has been rubbing my nose in stuff since he got me disqualified for the state tournament. I should have been on that podium. Not him." Mom wanted to say something about trying to bury the hatchet. That's PIDU4. She knew that was a stupid thing to say to an Indian. I'm not sure wrestling had anything to do with the hotel.

At least Dad wasn't sitting in the dark like he did when they let him go from Ketchikan Spruce. At least Dad was trying to fix Schumacher instead of me all the time. I don't think it was such a bad idea. At least he was trying something. Mrs. Greene would be happy. My biggest problem was trying to find the ghost of Frank Reid. He started the whole thing by messing up the construction site. HVI wasn't Soapy Smith as far as I could see. They just wanted to build a hotel.

The city council meeting wasn't until the end of the month. It was really dark in October. School was different when I got back. Before I bit Mr. Schumacher, the kids did the normal kind of ignoring. After I got back, they did that kind of ignoring where it feels like the air is sucked away from your body. They would try to stare without me noticing. They whispered and pointed until I walked by. I didn't even get called loser or nose-picker in the lunch line. In fact, Mrs. Clements took me to get my lunch first, so I could eat with her in the classroom. I wasn't five anymore. Mom worked hard so I could fit in. She told me all the special things I could do when I felt agitated by the noise.

It was hard to get through lunch every day with the birds flying in my head. Mom told me I had to practice at training the swarming bees to go back into their hives.

I did everything we talked about when I was little. I sat with my back to the wall so nobody could bump me and make me scream. I patted my knees under the table with my hand so that the bees could find a way to fly out of my body. That way I wasn't all the way agitated. I was even getting better at pretending that all of their conversations were like the Taiya River. You can all that one IWICP2 if you are starting your own glossary.

I thought I could keep trying. The first day back they all just parted and sat quiet like I was some kind of Frankenstein. For the first time, all of their whispers and quiet pushed the air around me. I tried my hardest but all I could do was put my head down and cry. The bees picked me up and swirled me around, and I was lost. Mrs. Clements came. She remembered not to touch me. She gave me the cough drop like Mom told her to do. The other kids ate their lunch and left. The air came back into the room. It was only Mrs. Warliss. She was Tlingit. She taught the little kids. She always rocked. I saw her. It was like her huge body was singing some song nobody could hear. I wish they saw me like that. Mrs. Warliss didn't try to talk. She wore totem patterns. Mrs. Clements went back to class. After I knew they were gone, I wiped my hand on my sleeve. I wiped my eyes with my fingers. I dried them on my jeans and took out my notebook. I tried to write things down, but the words flew away. My thoughts flew away. I took deep breathes like Mom told me to do. Mrs. Warliss didn't talk. She rocked even when she sat still. Nobody noticed. I took deep breaths. I sat and wrote in my notebook until it was almost time for school to be out.

"S'eek. Atk'átsk'u."

"I don't understand." I said. (You can label those IWICP3 and IWICP4.)

"I said Blackbear. I said Child."

"I'm not a baby," I sniffed.

"You okay to walk home, now?"

"I'm not a baby. Skagway isn't that b-b-ig." I was trying not to cry. I put my notebook away and walked out of the back of the cafeteria so nobody could see me in the hall. I wanted to prove to all of them that I was big. I went down to the construction site. Nobody was there. It was about to get dark.

"Frank Reid, I know you're out here. You have to help us. You got my dad put in jail the last time. That's not helping us. Now the kids think I'm a freak. That's not helping. I'm going to write more about you but you, have to start helping. My dad thinks the hotel is a bad thing. He doesn't want to move to Dyea. It's a ghost town. You must live there now. I don't want to live in a ghost town. Dad can't go to jail. He'll sit in the dark again. He'll try to fix me again. He stopped. Grandma Frampton made him promise when she died. He stopped!" I picked up a rock and threw it into the water where the gigantic ships dock during the summer.

I started to walk back home. Frank Reid heard me, I guess. I was almost back to Main Street when a huge explosion came from the construction site. I ducked behind the statue of Skookum Jim and watched. I got out my notebook. I made sure I had a good hiding place, so I wouldn't have to bite Mr. Schumacher if he found me. There was a shadow that ran past the flames and back up into the forest. I watched him run for a while. Everyone else was running toward the fire. I followed the shadow to the forest edge and hid again. Then I ran around the backside of the train station. I hid again while all the adults ran to the fire. I didn't want to get blamed. Then, right on the top of Kirmse's Curios Rock, a light flashed three times. It's the really old billboard they painted on the rock. It's pretty high up on the hill. They did it a long time ago. Right around the time Frank Reid killed Soapy Smith. All the tourists take pictures of it from the train station. I'm sure of it. I remember the important things. I know there were three lights that flashed. I had a story about Frank Reid's ghost. I had to have Mrs. Clements help me.

Chapter 11

"Hey Rockenstein." It couldn't be good. Rudy Schumacher was going to win state for wrestling. Dad said he had muscles for brains. It had been a couple of days. The explosion made the whole school buzz about HVI and the hotel. They were back to ignoring me in the normal way. I asked Mrs. Clements if I could try the cafeteria again. She was always tired. She said okay. I was busy writing everything I could in my notebook—about seeing the ghost of Frank Reid right before the explosion. Rudy sat down next to me. Nobody sat down next to me. I scooted away and kept writing. I tried to ignore him.

"You deaf too? I'm talking to you."

"There's a school paper that says you can't touch me."

"Easy, kid. Don't worry about it."

"I scream when people touch me."

"I hear you bite once and a while too." I looked up confused. I was definitely rocking. "I'd have given a million bucks to see the look on my old man's face when you bit him."

"I didn't mean too. There's a piece of paper. It tells people that they—."

"I heard. Nobody can touch you, Rockenstein."

"That's not my name."

"What is it, then Rockzilla? Rockinfella?"

"My name is Harold Reginald Blackbear Jones III"

"Yes, and my name is Rudolph Gregory Vincent Schumacher. Ever heard anybody call me Rudolph?"

"No."

"MMWLMSTW8 right! Last kid to call me Rudolph the Red Nose Reindeer ended up with a bloody nose. People call me Rudy. What do they call you?"

"People call me Rocky."

"Nice to meet you Rocky. Look I need to ask you a favor."

"I'm not good at favors. I only like vanilla."

"No. I mean that I need you to cover for me."

"Cover for me=PIDU5. I need to write that in my notebook."

"You always write in that notebook?"

"Yes. I don't understand what "Cover for me" means."

"It kind of means keep a secret."

"You're dad had my dad arrested. I don't like your secrets."

"Hold up, Rocky." Rudy looked over his shoulder. He kept talking. He pulled up his sleeve. He had a scar next to a huge purple spot on his arm. Then he leaned closer. I scooted away again. "Geez, hold still. I'm trying to level with you."

"Level with you=PIDU6."

"It means I'm trying to be honest. Now shut up before some teacher comes over here." I was quiet. I was rocking, but I was quiet. I wrote in my notebook.

"I'm listening. I listen when I write. People don't think so, but I listen when I write."

"Fine. Anyway, there's some kind of rumor going around that your old man had to move to Skagway because he got heat for beating on you back in Juneau."

"That's a lie. My dad just tries to fix me. He quit trying to fix me when Grandma Frampton died. She made him promise. Lots of parents try to fix their kids."

"MMWLMSTW, kid," Rudy whispered. "Um—well, see this mark?" I glanced up at him and nodded. "Well, this is my dad trying to fix me, like you said. Rocky, they're not fixing anything. They're just—."

"SCHUMACHER!" I jumped. The wrestling coach yelled like a gunshot.

"Yea, Coach!"

"That's a lie. My dad loves me. He sat in the dark a long time. He—."

"I gotta' go, kid. Do me a favor. Write more of those Frank Reid ghost stories."

"I'm going to. He's the one getting my dad in trouble."

"SCHUMACHER!" Rudy pulled his sleeve down. Rudy ran back to talk to his coach. His coach was looking at me when Rudy talked. He pointed. He shook his head. Rudy nodded. I finished my lunch. Rudy was nice. He didn't touch me. Mom said I needed to make friends. Maybe Rudy would be my friend. She said I needed to find someone that had something the same as I did. Rudy has someone trying to fix him. They must love him. I'm not sure. He frowned when I said that.

Friends help friends. I had to write my next ghost story. Mrs. Clements bit her lower lip when she saw what I wrote. "Are you sure about this, Harold?"

"I remember everything."

"It's just—. Why don't we make something up out of your imagination with werewolves or something?"

"I don't know anything about werewolves. I want to talk about Frank Reid and the explosion last night."

"That's just it. Principal Smith doesn't want you publishing anymore stories like this one. You understand. It's for your own good."

"But I worked hard on the story. Aren't you supposed to work hard on the story? That means people will want to read it."

"Harold, I know you worked hard on the story. I'm still going to give you a good grade. We just need you to write about something else for the school paper."

So I wrote something out of my imagination. I didn't have much to go on. I made some things up about black bears and a princess named Daphne. It wasn't really the Daphne in our school. I just picked the name. Maybe that was the real reason she threw the Shakespeare book at me when she got it. When I got home later that day, I asked my mom why she got so upset when I made her the princess in the story.

"The other girls got jealous."

"Jealous? Why?"

"Nobody is making them the princess."

"That's silly. It's probably because I rock."

"Eat your broccoli, Harold."

"I always do, Mom." Dad came in covered in dirt and ash. He didn't want them to think he blew up the lumber. He spent the day helping clean-up the explosion

"They painted "VANKERSLOOT=SON OF SOAPY" on one of the sheets of plywood. They were pretty serious. Used bolt cutters to slice through the chain link. They blew half the lumber to kingdom come. They tossed the rest of it off the dock." It took most all of us just to get the blaze under control. We're just lucky it didn't make it up the hill. We're lucky they were only starting to pour some footings before the weather sets in. If they'd had some framing lumber out there we might have had another 1899 on our hands." Dad's face was covered in soot. He was tired.

"It was the ghost of Frank Reid, Dad." I said. Mom told me not to aggravate him. She was mad enough that she couldn't find me right away when the explosion started. I didn't tell her that I was at the construction site.

"Not, now, Son. Whoever is doing this is going about it the wrong way. It just means they're going to come looking for some-body to blame if they can't get started. I don't want to be arrested again for things I didn't do."

"They'd never do that. You helped with the clean-up. You helped them put out the fire, just like everybody else."

"Doesn't matter. Why do you think I left Skagway to begin with? "

"They dropped those charges. Nothing was ever proven."

"They didn't have to prove anything. They did their damage. I was lucky to get that job at Ketchikan Spruce after that." I didn't want Dad to go sit in the dark. I tried to cheer him up. "Mrs. Warliss said Tlingit words to me today at school."

"Mary was always good at that. Even when we were kids. Maybe she can teach you to carve. Not many of them left around that can carve like Mary."

"I'd like that. I'll go write in my notebook. I won't get in trouble at school, Dad."

"Sounds good, Sport."

Chapter 12

I can see why Mrs. Greene was so upset. She came up on a long weekend. She invited our family over to Aunt Edna's for dinner. Aunt Edna had one of the oldest houses still standing in Skagway. She showed us pictures from the early 1900's. She showed us pictures when the town had about 9,000 people instead of 900. Aunt Edna had tons of little glass animals that she had collected over the years. Mrs. Greene wanted to make sure the house was donated to a museum when Aunt Edna didn't need it anymore. I hoped that was a long way away. She made awesome fried chicken and mashed potatoes. She even gave me my own glass of juice. Mom said it was okay this one time. It didn't have red dye in it. Not like the sugar drinks in the store. It was real juice.

"Why don't you live in Skagway anymore, Mrs. Greene?" We were all sitting around the table. Dad looked at Mrs. Greene and then back down at his soup. The table was draped with lace all over. Most of the time people only used lace on Sunday. Aunt Edna looked like she used it every day. Mom told me before we came that I was to keep my hands in my pocket unless we were eating. Aunt Edna was nice. She had a shelf just for old plates. The plates had pictures of places all over the world. The shelf had its own little fence to keep the plates in place.

"Because her heart was broken in Skagway," Aunt Edna said.

"Aunt Edna!" Mrs. Greene blushed.

"Well, good grief. Why don't you two quit pretending this is a normal situation? Tell the children before the three of you

58

adults explode." Mom said Aunt Edna never put on airs. Put on airs=PIDU7.

"It was a long time ago, Harold. Long before your dad met your mom. She's the best." I blinked at Mrs. Greene confused.

"You know how Daphne threw that book at you?" My mom said.

"Yes."

"Well, Mrs. Greene threw her lunch tray at your dad's head."

"You liked Mrs. Greene, Dad?" I wrinkled my nose.

"Something like that," Dad mumbled. He took a drink. "This soup is very good, Aunt Edna."

"Course it is, Harry. You don't get to be my age without learning how to make a good soup. Need something to warm your bones if you want to stick around here." Mom squirmed in her chair. Natalie giggled. "Now it seems that even though you two are all fired up about stopping that monster tourist complex, the rest of the town is in the middle. Some of them are right fine with getting a settlement and moving to the Dyea development Schumacher has tacked up on the wall at City Hall."

"I don't trust Schumacher," Dad said. "He's cheated before."

"High school is a long time ago," Aunt Edna sighed.

"I agree with Harry. Something just doesn't set right with this deal, Aunt Edna. Are you telling me you want to move?" Mrs. Greene said.

"Out of this drafty old house? Honey, I don't know. I love it quite a bit. Not sure a town should hold all its horses for one old lady."

"That's exactly why the town should hold its horses. We need to preserve who we are. We need to preserve all the history—." Tires squealed away. Metal crunched. Dad jumped up from the table. Natalie and I looked out the window to look at tail lights. Something dangled behind a pick-up truck.

"Stay inside!" Dad ordered. "*BOOM!*" Aunt Edna didn't listen. Like everyone in Skagway she had a gun. Aunt Edna wasn't as old as she looked. Her shotgun pelted the side of a barn right as the pick-up screeched around the corner.

"Jeez!" Mrs. Greene said.

"MMWLMSTW9." Aunt Edna. said. "Missed." Nobody listened to Dad. We all went outside to see what happened. Aunt Edna's house was old but her carport was not. It was new. Somebody hooked a corner of the carport to their pick-up truck. When they drove off the carport fell on Aunt Edna's car. We all stood in the cold.

"Why would they do that?" Natalie asked.

"Apparently the tribe isn't the only person giving them trouble." Mrs. Greene said. "Let's go back inside." We went inside. I started rocking. Mom asked if I need the big book. I shook my head no. I wasn't going to be a big baby. I was going to be big and listen to Mrs. Greene. Later on I was going to try and talk to the ghost of Frank Reid again at the construction site. I would talk in the dark while other people were eating dinner. The grown-ups didn't believe it. I think we needed the ghost of Frank Reid to help.

"Now, Aunt Edna, before I tell you, you need to put down Dad's pea shooter there—." Mrs. Greene started.

"Why? Did you do something stupid? Do I need to shoot you too?"

"Aunt Edna, just put down the gun."

"Fine. Harry you're going to have to give me a ride to work. Skagway Streetcar can't live a day without me on the phones."

"I'm sure they'll—."

"Or do you suggest I walk down Main Street waving my pea shooter until I find out who did this!" Aunt Edna growled.

"I'm happy to take you to work Aunt Edna. Now let's hear her out." Dad said. Aunt Edna went into the kitchen. She came back with some tea and cookies. She acted like shooting at a person was the same as swatting a fly. She was a strong lady. I kept rocking.

Mrs. Greene began, "When you first told me about this development I started investigating everything I could get my hands on about HVI. Harry was right. We can't trust them. Messing up the carport is just a warning. I filed an injunction with the state to investigate the deal. I hope it slows them down until we can find a real reason to stop them. We need more evidence."

"I can investigate." I said. I was still rocking. I started to pull out my notebook.

"Not this time, Sport." My dad was serious. I looked down at the table.

"The best thing you can do for us is to write down everything you see and hear in your notebook. If we need something we can ask." Mrs. Greene agreed with Dad. I didn't look up from the table. Natalie was leaning on her elbow and stirring the peas around her plate.

"Harry, don't pick me up for work tomorrow."

"Of course I'm going to pick you up."

"No such thing. The cowards will think they got to me. Rocky, how about you escort me to work."

"Not on your life, Aunt Edna," Dad said.

She stomped her foot. "MMWLMSTW8. I'm not some little snowflake that's going to melt. I need Rocky to go with me to remind me not to shoot Schumacher when we walk by his store."

"I'm not so sure," my mom said. I looked at Aunt Edna. I was a little taller than she was.

"That's the best idea I've heard yet," my dad said. He smiled at Aunt Edna. "Sport, you'd better make sure she doesn't put that pea shooter to her shoulder. She's a MMWLMSTW2 good shot."

"Well, while we're making plans, Aunt Edna——." Mrs. Greene looked down at the table.

"Well spit it out. What."

"I need to come live with you this summer."

"Why?"

"I kind of sold my house and cashed in all my savings to pay for the court fees."

Aunt Edna shook her head. She put her right hand to her mouth. He shoulders crumpled. "No, child. That was——."

"Not another word. You mean everything to me. I'm not going to let Schumacher bully you out of your home."

"What do you mean bully her out of her home?" Dad asked.

"Hush, Monica." Aunt Edna told Mrs. Greene. She didn't listen. Sometimes adults listen less than kids do at school.

"Schumacher has been coming around serving her papers and every kind of legal rot he can dig up to get her to sell her house. They can start the hotel, but it's kind of a bluff. Technically, if they can't relocate all the residents, then they can't complete the project. They have check points on the money and when the construction workers get paid."

"So Schumacher is going around trying to strong arm everybody?"

"He seems to have a bottomless pit of cash. He's already paid off most of the town on the sly."

"Well, we should do something so he can't sneak around!" Dad spouted.

"That's what I've been doing. Thanks to your stunt in the principal's office, the tribal lawyer is pitching in a little bit of help. We're starting to get to Schumacher."

"I should clean Schumacher's clock," Dad growled.

"That's what he wants you to do," Mom said.

"What do you mean?" Mrs. Greene asked.

"If Dad takes the blame, then Mr. Schumacher looks like a good guy," I said. I kept rocking.

"Very good, Harold," Aunt Edna said.

"He's not a good guy. He tries to fix Rudy the same way Dad used to try and fix me. Dad quit. Dad is a good guy. Mr. Schumacher didn't. He's not a good guy." The room got really quiet. Finally, Aunt Edna patted me on the wrist.

"You're right. Your dad is a good guy." When she patted me on the wrist it only screamed a little. More like just yelled than screamed. She patted my wrist kind of soft.

Chapter 13

"Hey Rockapalooza!"

"My name is Rocky." Rudy smiled. I don't understand teasing. Mom said that if they smile then they are teasing. She had to change her mind. By third grade she gave me three rules for teasing. I wrote them down.

1) If people are not smiling and they say something mean they are just being mean.

2) If people are smiling but you don't know them then the comment might be mean.

3) If people are smiling and they are your friends, then most of the time it's called teasing.

Now you see why all the rules float around like fish. As far as I can know Rudy was my first friend. We didn't talk on the phone. He just wasn't mean. He talked to me at lunch when the coach wasn't looking. That's a friend. Mom and all the doctors were big on me having friends. Mom didn't have any friends that I could see. She just took care of us. She worked when she could. She took me to my appointments. Other moms played soccer at my old school. They called them soccer moms. I never saw them play. My mom wasn't a soccer mom.

"Earth to Rocky." Rudy was waving his hands. I was writing in my notebook. I decided to ask.

"When you change my name, is that called teasing?"

"Uh, yea, kid. Listen. I don't have much time."

"When you get time could you write down those other names?"

63

"Sure, kid, it's just that I——."

"That way I can start a new glossary."

"Rocky." He grabbed my shoulders. I jumped and squeaked. He let go. I scooted away. I rocked faster. "Sorry, Buddy. Sorry. I forgot. In wrestling we're always grabbing some guy."

I was breathing pretty fast. He kept talking. "Can you hear me? Please don't freak out on me, kid." I nodded my head. It was shallow breathing like I needed an inhaler. I didn't need an inhaler. I didn't want to lose my friend.

"I just wondered why you didn't print the ghost story about Frank Reid? That Daphne and the bear thing was just kid's stuff. My buddies and I have this thing. We need the ghost of Frank Reid."

"The ghost just gets us all into trouble. Now Aunt Edna's car is smashed. It wasn't Frank Reid's ghost. It was somebody else driving a pick-up."

"I know, I——."

"SCHUMACHER!" The coach's voice hit the wall like a basketball thrown at my head. I ducked.

"Yea, Coach! Gotta' go. Write down all that you can about the ghost. Please. Keep it to yourself." Rudy got up and trotted over to the coach. His knee bumped the bottom of the table. My pear slices dribbled a little. That was okay. Mom says sometimes it's an accident. I didn't really like the sticky on my fingers. The sticky made me start to rock. It was okay. He was my friend. He didn't mean to. It was still sticky. Mom said it was okay to wipe it on my pants. She said my head would quit catching fire if I just wiped it on my pants. She said to imagine a magic bucket of water. It took some effort. I wiped it on my pants. I waited for the bucket of water to slow down my rocking. I didn't notice that all the kids were gone.

"S'eek?"

"Hi, Mrs. Warliss."

"You okay? It's time to go back to Mrs. Clements' class."

"I'm fine. I had to pour a bucket of water on my head to get the pear sticky off my fingers." She shook her head.

"Well, let me get you back to class."

"I can walk. I'm not a baby." She waited for me to pack my bag. I bumped my knee under the table. It was an accident. I rubbed my knee, and we started walking.

"I know you can, Honey. This is more for me, than it is for you. I hear you've been doing an awesome job escorting Mrs. Greene's aunt to work in the morning."

"Yes. I'm not sure she needs me. She walks great and nobody bothers her with that shotgun in her hand. Why is Mr. Schumacher here again?" This was like any school. All the offices had big windows. That's probably why they write so many rules. All the people in the office look like their heads are bobbing up and down. Just like the fish. That's why their rules always just float around and make no sense.

"Oh, he's just here trying to cause trouble again."

"Yea, but that's my dad and mom. Mom looks upset. Dad looks mad."

"Don't worry about——."

"And that's Rudy!" I broke away from Mrs. Warliss and pounded on the glass to get Rudy's attention. He glanced up and then glanced at his dad. Then he stared at the ground and nodded for me to go away. I knew what that meant. Mr. Schumacher was trying to fix something again.

"Come along, S'eek." Mrs. Warliss knew she couldn't touch me. She kind of herded me as if she was one of those huge cruise ships that came in and out of town. I couldn't get around her. I gave up and kept walking. I started talking fast.

"Mrs. Warliss, he's my friend. Mrs. Warliss, his dad tries to fix him. Somebody has to stop it, Mrs. Warliss." Mrs. Warliss looked up and down the hallway. She waited for me to quiet down and then sat me down on a bench to help me to stop rocking before I went into Mrs. Clements' room. It was art time, and so it was loud. I missed the quiet reading time. That's the best time for me to enter the classroom. I get too agitated when it is loud.

"S'eek. Harold. You have to understand that sometimes you can't go around blurting."

"He's my friend."

"I know he's your friend, but there are things you just can't change in the world. You know Skagway is special. It has deep waters. You can't change these deep cold waters. If you fall in there, you'll get hurt. Do you follow me?"

"Mr. Schumacher is deep cold water? He mostly looks like Santa Claus without all the laughing. He looks like Santa with no friends. He looks like Santa with no elves."

"You just need to listen to the adults. Take your nice walk with Aunt Edna. Do what your mother says. Do what your father says. Maybe we can start those carving lessons soon. What would you think of that?" I pulled out my notebook and tried to ignore her. She let out a deep sigh. "Can you sit out here with your notebook until Mrs. Clements is ready for you?" I should have said something, but I just started to write in my notebook. Mrs. Warliss had to go watch the little babies. I'm not a little baby. I spent three years in first grade. I was done being in the first grade. I rocked. I wrote in my notebook. I would have to investigate. Mrs. Clements must have forgot I was there. I wrote in my notebook for the rest of the day. When all the students started pouring into the hallways, I just ran out the front door so I wouldn't be run over. I ran all the way to the Skagway Streetcar Company where Aunt Edna worked.

Mrs. Greene and mom said I could go over there as long as I stayed out of the way. It was a business. Since it was slower during the winter time, her office was a little like a library. Mom made me promise to wear my earmuffs if the noise got too loud in the office. I promised. Aunt Edna didn't make me feel bad. You could tell she was related to Mrs. Greene. Mrs. Greene said she was a school teacher back when Skagway had more people. She said most of the people in town learned their ABC's in her room. She taught the babies. She doesn't treat me like a baby.

"Hello, Harold." Aunt Edna smiled when I came in. She set me up at one of the desks they didn't use during the winter. It was like being a grown-up in Mrs. Greene's library. It had a phone I wasn't supposed to touch. Aunt Edna said it was a business, so I had to work on being quiet. I wrote in my notebook. I filled it with descriptions of people in town. I filled it with conversations. People didn't think I was listening when I was rocking.

Aunt Edna was an important person. She answered all their phone calls. She was very polite no matter who was on the phone.

"I understand, but—." She said that 37 times one day. Many people interrupt what she is saying. The day Mr. Schumacher was at the school with Rudy, her face turned pink and the she laid her head on her desk when she hung up. I went out to see if she was okay.

"Why yes, Harold. That's kind of you to ask. I'm just a little under the weather."

"What did they say on the other line?"

"What do you mean?"

"Whatever they said turned your face different colors."

"You are as sharp as a tack, you are." She smiled. Sharp as a tack=PIDU 8. "It's nothing that my rheumatiz medicine can't cure when I get home. My boss Julie is in Juneau this week. Paul said he can't service car number 12 until he gets a certain part. Why don't we have you escort me a little early, today?"

"Sounds great." I put my earmuffs in the drawer. I put on my coat and back pack. Aunt Edna put on her coat and picked up her gun. We started to walk. I pulled my hood over my ears.

Aunt Edna waved her shotgun a little. "Most of the time I'm just trying to scare the birds. Now what you're about to see, you leave to old ladies. You never, never try this, you understand? You know I only have salt loaded in here." Aunt Edna leaned over to me like it was a secret. I turned and half my face was in my hood. My ear stuck out. I nodded my head. "In fact, you stay right here and watch from behind that tree. Then you can keep escorting me around the corner on 3rd. Okay?" I pulled my hood back so I could see. I nodded again. Aunt Edna walked up to Mr. Schumacher's store. She waited just inside that strange overhang like she was a real-life spy on a TV show. Her shotgun was pointed in the air. Then right when Mr. Schumacher stepped out of his shop to get in his truck she pulled the trigger.

"MMWLMSTW5! MMWLMSTW7, MMWLMSTW3, MMWLMSTW4!" Mr. Schumacher did a belly flop into the dirt. He looked all around to see who was shooting.

Aunt Edna bent down and tapped him with the butt of her gun. "That was a warning, Ralph Henry Schumacher. Those phone calls are getting right tiresome from your fancy lawyers. Next time someone comes to my house, I might be a better shot. I taught you the ABC's. You need to be nicer to the class." People came running out of their shops to see where the gunshot came from. Aunt Edna turned around to all of them. "Gotta' stop being afraid of this nonsense. The weather around here is tough enough to cope with. We don't need any more complications. Need to work together."

She had that old-lady look. The one Mom uses when she's just lost it. The look warning her children to duck and be quiet if they wanted to keep their head. She walked around the corner. I caught up to her and finished walking her home.

"Thank you very much, Harold. You have been a perfect gentleman. I'd tell you that you should keep this a secret but Skagway is a pretty small place. I'm sure your dad already knows."

Chapter 14

Things got kind of quiet after that. Mr. Schumacher and his family took a weekend trip before Rudy started wrestling season. During wrestling season, the only thing Mr. Schumacher did was follow the team around the state screaming his head off at the refs. That's what Dad told me. Mom and Dad sat me down after Aunt Edna shot Mr. Schumacher. I mean after she scared him with her shotgun.

After dinner Natalie did the dishes. It was my job to help take them to the sink. Mom let me have my notebooks after I cleared the table. I worked fast. I got my notebook. This one was new. It was notebook number 110. That's not a prime number. Eleven is a prime number. Eleven times 10 equals 110. This one is blue like the first one Mrs. Greene gave me. "Sport, we need to talk." I kept writing. I started rocking. "I mean now, Sport." Dad didn't let my mind wander. I nodded and concentrated on getting my hand to stop writing. When Dad drives the car he has to concentrate on the brakes to make it stop. Mom says that he does it unconsciously. Unconsciously=PIDU 9. I have to concentrate on everything people want me to do. The only thing I don't have to concentrate on is writing in my notebook or flipping pages in my special book. Or rocking. I don't have to concentrate on rocking. "Now, Sport." Dad was keeping his temper in check. In check=PIDU 10.

"Harold." Mom was helping me.

"I'll stop writing now." I put my pen down. I didn't stop rocking.

"Can you hear me when you're rocking?" Dad asked. He was trying.

"Honey, you know that new friend you have?" Mom asked.

"Rudy. Rudy is my friend. He teases me. Rule number three on people being mean, Mom. Rudy only teases me. He smiles. Rudy is my friend."

"Sport, that's what we're here to tell you." It was silent. The air was starting to push in on me like every other time something is bad.

"Rudy is my friend. I saw you talking to Mr. Schumacher. He looked mad. Rudy looked at me, but he didn't smile."

"Yes, Honey. Mr. Schumacher forbids his son to talk to you. He came down to the school to complain. The coach saw him talking to you and complained."

"He came up to me. I didn't ask. I didn't let him eat my lunch. I eat my whole lunch. I'm hungry. Other kids let him eat their lunch. They pretend to be his friend. I didn't pretend. Rudy is my friend."

"Sport." Dad sighed and ran his fingers through his hair. He looked at the table. "Not everybody understands—."

"Rudy asked me to write more stories about the ghost of Frank Reid. Rudy understands. Mrs. Clements told me we couldn't publish them. I wrote another story, and now Daphne is mad. Rudy is my friend." I started to rock faster. The birds were fluttering and bees were starting to swirl.

"He's pitching a fit over this." My dad was mad. Mom came around and got on her knees to talk to me eye to eye.

"Here's your notebook. Why don't you write more stories in your notebook? Lord Dwark needs another dragon story. Remember?"

Dad stood up, angry. "You're babying him. World isn't going to coddle him, Lois. He'll need to face the Schumachers of the world. Can't baby him forever."

"I'm not a baby." I blurted. Dad spun around. Mom stood up. "Rule number three! Rudy is my friend. I'm not a baby." I grabbed the notebook and my pen. I focused on making the pen do what I wanted it to do. Dad stomped out of the room. Doors slammed. Mom followed him. They were arguing. I held onto the pen like I held onto that tree branch when I was five. I climbed up into this tree. Nobody called me Rocky. I wasn't in school. I climbed the tree and Mom told me to come down. Isaac across the street dared me to climb the tree. I wasn't a baby. I did a good job. I just got stuck in one place. Mom was washing dishes and didn't look up. I held on and held on to that branch. Finally, I had to let go because my arms wiggled from being too weak. It hurt my ankle a little bit. Not much. I just limped. My pen was that branch every day. I try not to rock. My brain gets tired trying. Just like my arms got tired trying to hold on.

In my next story Lord Dwark finds the tree people. They always live in the trees. They never come down. They are happy. The have enough food. They have libraries in the trees, and the kids have special playgrounds on big trees. Mrs. Greene lives in the tallest tree. Mom and Mrs. Greene are the queens of the tree people. They help the kids learn to always live in the tree. Lord Dwark smiles when he visits. He can't stay. The tree people feel sorry for him.

There was a low rumble from Mom and Dad's bedroom. Dad's low voice. Mom's loud voice. They were fighting again. They would fight a long time. Sometimes it is about me. Sometimes it is about the stack of bills and waiting lists. I know how to put myself to bed. That makes it easier on Mom. On a good night they only fight an hour. Then Mom does the dishes. On a bad night they fight longer and Dad stomps out the back door. They think I don't hear them. I remember the important things. I have an hour now. I can go talk to Frank Reid at the construction site. I can tell him that Dad needs a job. Grandma Frampton didn't leave as much food behind as we thought. They will think I'm in bed. I will sneak around the dark like a spy on TV.

The door closed with a creak. I had my hat and gloves on. I had the flashlight Dad kept by the circuit breaker for when the power went out. I had my notebook and pen. In the dark I looked normal. Nobody could see me rock. It's almost as good as being one of the tree people that Lord Dwark visited. They told me to make friends. When I made a friend, they told me to not talk to him. The coach didn't like me. I don't know why. I didn't talk to the coach. I didn't wrestle. It was easy to get to the construction site. It was quiet.

I yelled, "Frank Reid!" Everything was quiet. They had a power pole and a new sign. "You need to help save the town, Frank Reid! Just like last time!" There was an owl that answered me. I think it was telling me to go home. *P-Ting! Zing!* The lights went out on the pole. With my flashlight I looked at the sign. The letters screamed. They were all capital. "24 HOUR VIDEO SURVEILLANCE COURTESY OF HVI." There was another *P-Ting! Zing!* Something made the dirt go poof five yards away from me. The last time I saw that Aunt Edna decided to unload her shotgun at a squirrel running behind her fence. Someone was shooting. *P-Ting! Zing! Zing!* They were shooting at the pole again. I could hear them. I would have to write it in my notebook later. I needed to sneak back home. They saw me.

Just like the fourth of July, the grey cylinder attached to the pole exploded. It smelled like burnt squirrel. One by one the lights in Skagway went out. It was really dark. Mom and Dad would need the flashlight. I would be in trouble soon. I still ran. Something stung my leg.

I tripped up the back steps with my flashlight bouncing. "HERE YOU GO!" I was out of breath. I handed it to Mom.

"Where have you been?!" Mom was between me and Dad.

"You were fighting, and I thought I had an hour before I went to bed and—." Dad snatched the flashlight.

"GO TO YOUR ROOM!" He yelled. I ducked and ran to my room. I slammed the door. I turned on the light and wrote down everything I remembered. I didn't notice the throbbing at first. I didn't want to get in more trouble. I just kept writing. I would prove that I wasn't a baby. I wrapped my leg with a bunch of old socks. Mom would be mad. She would have to get me new socks. It was throbbing more. It felt like the wasp sting I had that summer when I was seven. Only the wasp had fire on its stinger. The wasp had a stinger on fire and was the size of a raccoon.

I tied it around my leg and kept writing. I wrote about the tree people being attacked by a wasp the size of a raccoon. They weren't strong enough to stay in the trees, and they were getting dizzy. I remember once when my leg hurt after my ankle swelled up, they told me to put it in the air. I tied the socks on tighter and above the wasp sting laid on my back and kept writing. Luckily the tree people had a way to cut down some old trees. They wove a gas mask for everybody out of the twigs and started the tree on fire under some damp moss. It made a big smoky mess. They had to have their fire-fighting tree people make sure it didn't light the whole forest. There was a knock on my door.

"Harold?" I guess they were done fighting.

"Yea, Mom."

"Can I come in?"

"Yea, Mom." She came in slow and screamed. I jumped, and it made my leg throb and hurt more. "What did you do?!" I was getting too dizzy. I just pointed to my leg. Dad rushed in.

"What the MMWLMSTW3?" Dad looked at my leg. My pants were soaked. There was blood everywhere. "We've got to get him to Dave. Last year Benny got shot hunting. Dave took care of it. Hey, Sport. You need to stay with us." I nodded. I went back to writing. "You understand? Does the writing help?" I nodded. Dad picked me up and Mom picked up my notebook.

"I didn't want to worry you. I tried to put on a band aid. I don't want to be a baby."

"You did good, Sport. You did good. Just keep writing. Don't fall asleep just yet. Just keep writing."

"Sorry about the sheets, Mom." She was opening the car door. Natalie was rubbing her eyes. She had her blanket and started whining, pulling into a tight ball and staying asleep in the seat next to me.

"Don't talk, now. We'll figure it out."

Chapter 15

"That's one MMWLMSTW4.5 strong kid you got there, Harry. You want a necklace made out of the slug?" Dave was the pharmacist. He was a medic in Vietnam and knew my grandfather Harold Reginald Blackbear Jones. I'm going to name my son something different. Dave took care of emergencies. If something was really bad, they called a helicopter to get us to Juneau. Mom had too many bills and waiting lists, so we were trying to have Dave help us.

"No, I need to check something out. Look like a .22?"

"Yea. Kind of a weird one. Harry, you know this is bad. There were no lights. Who's going around with a night scope?"

"Don't know, Dave."

"Schumacher is going to have a MMWLMSTW2.5 fit." Dad just looked outside. "Well, I've wrapped the wound with some antibiotics. You should catch the ferry tomorrow to Juneau and get it checked at a hospital."

"And say what? My autistic son got shot in a hunting accident? That will go over well."

"You could try the truth. He was wandering around where he wasn't supposed to be, and some idiot with a night scope started shooting up the construction site."

"Not sure that will set much better."

"Suit yourself. He does need to be seen." Dave looked at me. "You're just lucky the shooter was so far away. He could have hit him in the head and we'd be planning a funeral."

74

"The ghost of Frank Reid was helping me." I said. I was rocking and writing my notebook. I didn't look up.

"Well I'm sure he did, Harold. That's all I can do. Watch him really close. Feed him some liver to get his iron back up." I wrinkled my nose. Dave smiled. "Well, then just feed him something. Whatever you do, Harry figure out a story and get him checked out. We need you back here for that city council meeting. It stands to be a doozy after this one. Does Edna have a back-up generator?"

"I think so. Not sure."

"I'll go check on her. Good night, Harry. Goodnight Lois. You keep writing, Harold. Goodnight Natalie." I nodded and kept writing. They cut the pants off of me earlier. The blood was sticking to everything. Mom washed me up and had me put on my gym shorts. My knees were bony. There was a white bandage wrapped below my right knee on my calf. I don't know why that part of your leg is named after a cow. It doesn't make sense.

"How are you feeling?"

"It throbs quite a bit. Not like the raccoon wasp stinger when it first happened. Still hurts." Mom had me sleep on the couch in the living room next to the wood stove. Dad cleaned up all the messy sheets and blankets in my room. Mom sat in the chair next to me and turned to read a book. Dad and Natalie headed to bed. "Sport?"

"Yea, Dad."

"You are one tough kid." I nodded and kept writing.

In the morning my leg was too stiff to move. It throbbed and hurt. Mom fed me breakfast and got some baggy sweat pants out of the closet for me to wear to Juneau. Dad wrapped us all up and put on his floppy dog ear hat. It's red plaid on the outside. It's furry on the inside. Dad ties the ears up over on top of his head when he doesn't need them. Dad mostly lets them flap. He looks like a poodle. I don't tell him that. I just write it down. We didn't talk much during the trip. Natalie went to stay with Aunt Edna to keep her company. Mom told Natalie to keep Aunt Edna inside and away from her shotgun. Natalie's eyes got wide but she nodded and went inside. I wanted the cookies I smelled baking in the kitchen. Aunt

Edna said when I got back she would bake me my own batch. I nodded and made a note of it.

The ferry ride felt slow. I concentrated on the writing and the throbbing. Mom got us seats next to the window in a quiet section. Dad unwrapped our snacks, and we munched on sandwiches. I was just glad it wasn't the tourist season. Dad got antsy and picked up a Juneau Tribune. He pulled out the sports section and started reading. Mom picked up the rest of the paper and took a look.

"Oh, dear." She put her hand to her mouth. "Harry. Look at this."

Dad groaned. "How did they know? Dave wouldn't have told them."

"What?" I asked. They didn't answer. They finished reading. Mom handed me the article to copy into my notebook.

SKAGWAY VANDALS ESCALATE TO VIOLENCE

Rolling power outages went up and down the grid from Haines to Skagway last night when a transformer next to the HVI tourism complex site was destroyed. HVI has been in the process of developing a multibillion dollar complex to better serve the cruise lines. At this time no one at HVI can be reached for comment.

After two other minor incidents, the vandals used high powered rifles to destroy construction materials as well as the newly-installed video surveillance system. With a flare of imagination, the vandals spray painted "Soapy Smith" on key pieces of equipment. Sheriff Tate of Skagway says that there is an open investigation and that he cannot compromise that process at this time.

Skagway mayor Ralph Schumacher issued this statement. "We are saddened by this latest setback. With all progress we realized that there would be a few unhappy people. We just didn't know that the people trying to block this lovely facility would resort to such tactics." When further questioned about how much the vandalism delays construction, Mr. Schumacher reported that he was not aware that it would cause any major delays. Mr Schumacher said, "If I didn't know any better I would think it was a disgruntled former employee of one of the lumber mills that had shut down in recent years."

Mr. Schumacher concluded by saying that he is petitioning the state for more aid in apprehending the vandals so that progress can continue.

"Lois, you need to take this."

"What am I going to do with this?"

"If something goes wrong, I need to you get it to Monica. Tell her to get Walt to figure out exactly what kind of gun it came from."

"But——." I protested as mom took the bullet and tucked it in her purse.

"No buts, Sport." I nodded and kept writing. "I need you to write everything down from last night."

"I already did. I'm going to be a famous crime novelist." Dad smiled.

"Well, keep it up. And keep it to yourself. Don't try to publish it in the school paper anymore."

"Okay. Mr. Schumacher lied to the paper, Dad."

"I know, Sport."

"I think he lies quite a bit." Dad just nodded. When I write and nod, people think I'm ignoring them. When Dad nods, people just think he's thinking. I'm thinking when I write. That's why I write.

"How's the pain? Do you need more pain meds?" Mom asked. I shrugged.

"I'm okay. Dad should wear a fake beard and hide under the blankets so that he can sneak back to Skagway and catch the person shooting. The ghost of Frank Reid will help him find the person."

"Wish it was that easy, Sport." Dad looked sad. His voice started to sound like the birds flying away. Mom gave him that tired look she usually saved for the bills and waiting lists. I handed Mom the newspaper back after I copied a couple of more articles out of it on the weather report. I copied some columns of numbers out of the back page. I went back to writing about Lord Dwark and the tree people. When they used all the smoke to chase away the wasp, they found out that the old trees made the soil happy. Little trees grew out of the old trees. The little trees made a fence and asked the rest of the forest if they ever saw a wasp the size of a raccoon. They didn't mind normal raccoons. Normal raccoons were their friends.

They started making their announcements about us getting off the ferry. A man in a long black coat came up to our seat.

"Harold Reginald Blackbear Jones Jr.?" The man was wearing sunglasses inside. He didn't smile. Dad didn't smile.

"Yes."

"As a Marshall for the Department of Alaskan Transportation, I'm asking that you stay back with me while the other passengers depart."

"My son was shot last night."

"That is unfortunate but——."

"Sir, this is my family. I will go quietly, but I need you to take them to the hospital. I didn't do this."

"I'm staying with my dad." I said. I blurted it loud. I was rocking. People looked up.

"Harold, not now." My mother patted me on the knee three times to focus. I kept writing.

"I'm afraid we can't——."

"MMWLMSTW! I'M STAYING!" I kept rocking. The big man stepped back. My mom gave me stinky eyes. My dad just looked out the windows.

"You have a special needs son?" The big man asked. The big man must have been stupid. Dad wouldn't look at him.

Dad just whispered, "Never mind. Lois take care of him." The big man stood and stared. I screamed at him. Dad said, "You are bothering him." I screamed again. The big man stared. Dad just looked out the window. I started rocking. I started banging my head with my hands. I started growling with tears at the big man. Then I looked away and kept rocking. People were staring. The big man grabbed Dad's elbow. Dad yanked his elbow away and whispered, "Let's go before the whole boat blows your secret." They walked away. Everyone stared. I delayed the next boat. Mom gave me a cough drop. The ferry found someone with a car to take me to the hospital. Mom sat next to me and looked out the window. The nice lady taking us wanted to talk. Mom sat there like a statue. The nice lady did her best. I wrote in my notebook. My leg was throbbing again.

Chapter 16

They asked a ton of questions at the hospital. The man in the big coat came by with another man in a big coat. Mrs. Greene came to sit with me while the two men asked Mom questions in the next room. A social worker came next and did the same thing. The doctor didn't say much. He just checked boxes. Everyone kept telling me it was okay for him to touch me. He had huge nose hair. He smelled like soap and pipe tobacco. Mrs. Sydney, Aunt Edna's neighbor, smokes pipe tobacco like that. She said she did it to remember her dead husband Ryan. When the doctor looked in my eye with the light my head exploded with screaming. Mrs. Greene was holding my hand. It was almost as bad as the wasp sting I got from the bullet in Skagway. He said I was healthy as a horse other than the gunshot wound and the autism. Healthy as a horse= PIDU11.

"Autism isn't the same as a gunshot. There's a piece of paper at the school that says you can't touch me. Mrs. Greene said this wasn't school." I told him. He glanced at me and kept talking to his recorder. He was old. Mrs. Greene patted my hand three times. She must talk to Mom a lot. The doctor left.

"You okay?" Mrs. Greene asked.

"Autism is kind of like a being shot by a gun. It's just not the same. When people touch me it feels like a tiny gunshot. It hurts in a way I can't explain. It makes my skin scream. A gunshot goes away. Autism doesn't go away. They're not the same."

"No, Honey. They're not the same."

"Autism isn't a crime either. It feels like people want to put you in autism jail. That's why I'm going to be a famous crime novelist. Gunshots happen in crimes. Autism isn't a crime."

"No, Honey. It's not a crime," she said with that quiet voice that made the birds fly away.

After I got shot, Aunt Edna brought Natalie on the ferry the next weekend. It was almost Thanksgiving. Natalie smiled at me. She had the same eyes as Mom. Tired and blue. She was learning that thing Mom did where she was nice to me in a flat faraway place. It was like we were talking through three sheets of glass. We could say everything perfect and still feel like we were on the telephone with me here and Natalie was in Seattle. We weren't in Seattle. We were in Juneau. Luckily Mrs. Greene had a friend with an empty apartment near the hospital they let Aunt Edna and Natalie stay at while Mom waited for me to get out. When I got out, they let us stay there while I recovered.

For Thanksgiving Aunt Edna came down and cooked for all of us. "The turkey smells really good, Mrs. Greene."

"Thank your mom, Rocky. Remember, I can't cook." Mom tried to smile. We were spending Thanksgiving in Juneau. Mrs. Greene was visiting the little apartment too. With things the way they were, Aunt Edna said it was probably safer if we stayed with her for a while until things blew over. Schumacher was making a big show of the whole thing. He even invited the governor to the ribbon cutting at the HVI site come spring. "Just like Soapy Smith." I told her. She smiled when I told her that.

The apartment was crowded. Mrs. Greene set up a chair and put the word Rocky on it in first grade teacher letters. I knew I could sit there. Mom gave me my pills every day at seven in the morning. After I took my pills Mom said to write in my notebook if something wasn't right in the schedule. Ever since the third grade I wrote it down if something wasn't on schedule.

The only time it didn't work was with Mr. Clausen in third grade. After he took my special book, he took my notebook one day. For the rest of the day I looked at his big schedule on the board. I yelled every time we were late. "IT'S READING TIME. IT'S 10:15.

WE'RE LATE." By the third time we were late, I was in the principal's office. He didn't give me my notebook, so I just yelled the time every time a bell rang. Mrs. Greene came and got me.

"Rocky, where is your notebook?" She asked.

"He said I had to pay attention like everyone else. He took it. Mom said to write in it if something wasn't right in the schedule. I was supposed to write down the time instead of shouting it. Mrs. Martinez tried it once too. Mom had to have a meeting. Mom needs to have a meeting." Mrs. Greene was giving the clock stinky eyes.

"Wait right here." She came back with my notebook and special book. Her lips were really thin, and she wouldn't talk. She didn't smile either. We went back to the library, and I got all the way to the letter "H" in my special book before the end of recess. She told the other kids stories about dinosaurs. We had the big meeting with Mr. Jacobs the next week. My leg hurt but I was glad I wasn't in Mr. Clausen's class anymore.

Thanksgiving was fun. Aunt Edna told stories about when Mr. Schumacher was little and we laughed. For instance one day he got into a huge fight. A big Tlingit kid named Bobby tried to pick on Mr. Schumacher. "Poor Bobby didn't know that Ralph's great-grandmother was Tlingit. He had the blood flowing in his veins. He got hopping mad. Harold did you know that the Tlingit drove out the Haida before Skookum Jim was even a glint in his father's eye?" I nodded. Glint in his father's eye=PIDU12. "Ralph knew his calling was wrestling that day. I remember having to pull Ralph by the collar to get him off poor Bobby. Ralph is just a hothead."

"Well he's a grown up now. He should control his temper and stop shoving us around."

"Monica, Dear. Let's not spoil our digestion with that talk." I didn't know Mrs. Greene's first name was Monica. You never learn a teacher's first name in school. It felt strange to see Mrs. Greene turn her head to that name, and I was embarrassed like I accidently saw somebody's underwear in the grocery store when they bent down to get a can of peas. Aunt Edna kept talking. "Don't you worry. Ralph always steps in poop and then pretends it's not on his shoes. Something will work out." Everyone got kind of quiet and finished eating. We were too full for the pumpkin pie right away so we helped Mom with the dishes. It was my job to clear the table. My gunshot wound was getting way better. I limped a little, but I didn't want them to notice so I stopped using the crutches early. I didn't want Mom to have more bills and waiting lists. When I was done with my part, I went to my chair and put on my earmuffs. They were going to watch football as if Dad was home. Dad was in jail. Mom missed him and said the football game was his favorite part. I always put on my earmuffs when the TV was on. I can't concentrate on my notebooks, and when someone gets a touchdown I want to yell. More like a screech. I just want to screech to make the sounds stop. At our house I could go to my room. Here I had to use the earmuffs. It was okay because my family didn't look at me like a retard. They ignored me the way a family ignores everyone in the family. We all ignore that Dad snores. It's okay. We all ignore Natalie when she acts like a brat and says she won't eat turkey. It's okay. We all ignore Mom when she cries in the kitchen a little. It's okay. It felt okay when they ignored me.

There wasn't as much shouting at the touchdowns. The rest of the night was nice, and after the pie I asked if I could go to bed. Mom, Mrs. Greene and Aunt Edna gave me a really faraway look. I didn't want the air to start pushing up against me. It was a good day. I knew I was going to bed before my schedule said to go to bed. I didn't care. Mom just nodded. I had dreams about Frank Reid coming into town and wrestling Mr. Schumacher for the state championship. I'm not sure who won.

The next day Mom sat me down at the table with Aunt Edna and Mrs. Greene. They looked serious. They looked like this was a special school meeting without us being in school.

"Harold we need to talk." I was writing. I nodded. Mom was quiet. She had been crying. Mrs. Greene kept talking. "Do you remember those men at the hospital?" I nodded. "Do you remember all of those times that I had to sit with you while your Mom went and talked to other official people?" I nodded and kept writing. "Well they don't understand you as well as we do and, well——." Now Mrs. Greene was crying.

"The official people are from child services. They had anonymous complaints against your family. They don't think your parents are taking good enough care of you." Aunt Edna finally said in a low voice.

"They don't have any kids with autism. Anonymous doesn't really mean 'not identified by name.' It means people are too chicken to say their names. The dictionary is wrong. My special book is wrong. That's why I just flip the pages. You adults always screw up the definitions." I didn't look up. I just kept writing.

"Well, Harold, I think you are absolutely correct. The thing is that they have this file on you now, and they want to keep investigating."

"What does the file say?"

"It says that your Dad isn't a good guy. It says your Dad is in jail and quit his job. It says you haven't been to school in three weeks. It says your family doesn't watch you close enough. Some of them think the gunshot wound came from a family member."

I kept writing Mrs. Greene had a fish tank. All we could hear was the filter running and the furnace going *ping, ping.* The words were starting to scramble, and I was trying to breathe. Everybody knew that being quiet helped me.

"So why is Mom crying. What do we have to do?"

"Well she got a letter that says they are going to investigate your family for the next 90 days. If the official people with the state don't like what they see, they will take you to a different place that takes care of autistic people all the time."

"They want to put me in autistic jail." I kept writing. Natalie was in her room playing. A car drove by. I was glad they were quiet. I wasn't sure what to do next. I wasn't agitated. I wish I could tell people that the rules float around. I looked up at the fish tank. I get upset when other people are loud and upset. I get agitated when I don't understand. I don't get agitated when I don't understand but my schedule is correct. I don't get agitated when I take my pills at seven. It was 7:30 when we were talking. They let me write in my notebooks. They were all quiet. We all looked at the fish tank a while. The fish don't have autism. They just float around. Nobody tells them not to float. Aunt Edna cleared her throat. Tears were going down Mom's face. "Yes, Honey. If they don't like what they see at the end of 90 days then they want to put you in autistic jail."

"So we need to pretend everything is okay like Frank Reid pretended to inspect the businesses." I said.

"Something like that."

"Are they going to let Dad out of jail for us to pretend?"

"We're not sure, Honey. We're not sure." I went back to writing in my notebook. I wrote down the time. Writing down the time helped my schedule. Notebooks don't help all the autistic kids. Other kids wear the earmuffs like the other Harold wore a helmet. We're not stupid.

"I don't want to go to autistic jail. I want to stay with Mom. I'll go back to Mrs. Clements' class and pretend to inspect the businesses. I'm going to be a famous crime novelist someday." Aunt Edna smiled. She patted my shoulder three times. I was focusing just fine. I had my meds. She didn't need to tap me three times. They were letting my mind wander. It was quiet. I was focused. She didn't need to tap me three times. That was okay. She said that Mr. Schumacher would step in something.

Chapter 17

"Welcome back." Mrs. Clements smiled. Mrs. Greene took a few days off of her job to come help us settle back in at Skagway. All the people smiled at us when we came back. The kids were back to ignoring me like they did when the air pushes in around me, and they whispered and pointed. Mrs. Clements had me eat lunch in her room for the first few days. Aunt Edna convinced her bosses that Mom needed a job, so they let her clean the office twice a week. Dave, at the pharmacy, let her be a clerk one day a week. She did inventory. There wasn't much to do in Skagway in December. Mrs. Clements tried to work it out with Mr. Smith to make Mom a teacher's aide or cafeteria lady but he said it wasn't in the budget.

Dad was still in jail when we moved back. His tribal lawyer was doing the best that he could, but there were different people involved with the situation. He said the system can be a hair clog. He told Mom a teenager spent three years in prison in New York before they figured out he didn't do anything. That made her cry. I don't know why the lawyer told her that. About a week before Christmas break, they let me try the cafeteria again. Mrs. Warliss came in earlier than usual to check on me and that was okay because she didn't treat me like a baby. After school I went to her room when the little kids had gone home. She showed me how to hold some of the carving tools. She told me stories about the bears and the otters she was carving. She was like everyone in Skagway. She had to make piles and piles of bears and otters to sell to the tourists. After a couple of days

85

of letting me write in my notebooks, she got my attention and put something in my hand.

"Here." She handed me a little carving that was half finished. "This is your own little black bear, S'eek."

"It's not done." I put it down and went back to my notebook and started writing. She stopped me.

"S'eek. This is you. You are just half-finished."

"I'm going to be a famous crime novelist. I know——." She handed me the carving again.

"This is a gift. You are unique. The rest of us have to be polished. We're the same. I have to make all of these bears the same, so the tourists will buy them. It makes me sad. We have carved for generations. Each totem was unique. Unique like you are unique. You put that one in your pocket. When you are ready, you can finish it. Can you help me put these in boxes?" Sorting her creatures was like sorting books for Mrs. Greene, only there weren't letters and numbers. There were just different kinds of shapes. I loved matching the shapes to the boxes. She was a really great carver. She was really fast. Dad was right. When I was done sorting, I stopped to watch her. She was humming. She rocked. She didn't care if I rocked. It looked like she didn't care if I was there. She was just making these animals appear almost as fast as Mom could peel a potato. Then she would pick up other tools and bring the bear to life. I looked up at the clock and saw that Mom might be late. I went back to my notebook and wrote down the time. Lord Dwark went further on his journey and came to a land where giant black bears were having a party. They were dancing and drinking egg nog because it was Christmas. The bears were laughing, but Lord Dwark was afraid when he came to the entrance of their cave. All he heard was growling and roaring. He thought the bears were supposed to be sleeping. It turned out he walked through the wrong entrance to the cave and was in their dream room. The bears slept so long that it took a different cave to hold their dreams. Lord Dwark didn't know it. He saw the Northern Lights flash on the cave wall. Purple and green flashes with stars on the ceiling of the cave as bright as the newer flashlights the hunters use at night.

"Harold." Mom was there. She wasn't that late. "Say Thank you to Mrs. Warliss."

"Thank you to Mrs. Warliss." I said, putting my notebook away.

"Harold." Mom gave me half a stinky eye. She didn't mean it. Mrs. Warliss smiled.

"Thank you, Mrs. Warliss."

"You are very welcome, S'eek." We left her room. It sounded like a herd of elephants. It turned out it was the wrestling team running laps. The school had hallways that formed a rectangle. The wrestling team ran in the hall because it was bigger than the wrestling room. The high school basketball team was using the big gym. The high school wrestling team ran here in the middle school. We all ate in the same cafeteria. Mom and I stayed out of the way. I saw Rudy run by but he was dripping in sweat. He didn't see me. Mom and I walked outside to go home. "Rudy is my friend. He doesn't talk to me anymore. He frowns when he sees me."

"For now, that's probably best. You'll find some new friends. It looks like Mrs. Warliss is your friend."

"She's a grown-up. That doesn't count. She takes care of the babies."

"Well there's the recreation center. She teaches carving there to the kids that want to learn. Why don't we take you there? Maybe you could make friends there."

"Just so there's no babies there. I'm going to be a famous crime novelist. I don't want to be with babies."

"Well, class is this next Saturday. I'll go with you."

"You can't have a special meeting with people before." I told her.

"What do you mean?" The mist was coming up from the canal. It was dark.

"People either ignore me or they smile too big after the special meeting. I just want to go. I'm used to people staring."

"Okay, we'll try it and see." We made it home, and Natalie was there starting dinner. She was younger than me but they let her use the stove. She only started dinner when Mom was working late or at an appointment with me in some doctor's office. Mom spent her days off cleaning Grandma Frampton's house until it looked like a museum. She wanted to buy new curtains, but the pay she was getting didn't let us do much more than eat. I ate all the school lunch, but it was never enough food. Mom made sure we had enough food.

Things weren't as sad as Thanksgiving. Mom was getting to know different people. Dad's family had been in Skagway for as long as Aunt Edna. Mrs. Warliss was just Mary to Mom. She was one of Dad's cousins or something. Some days Aunt Edna let Mom answer the phones. She was always teaching people something. Skagway Streetcar was only paying Mom to clean, but they seemed happy that Aunt Edna was teaching someone else about the phones. The bosses said the phones were going to catch fire pretty soon. Phones catch fire pretty soon=PIDU13. Dad wasn't out of jail yet but Dad and Mom were able to write back and forth.

The carving class turned out to be good. Daphne was in class. There were only two other kids and one of them got bored and quit. Mrs. Warliss didn't yell or give us a bunch of rules other than the baby obvious ones about knives and chisels being sharp. I liked carving. Our bears and otters looked simple. Mrs. Warliss was using bigger chisels to make the raven and salmon carvings with the traditional Haida and Tlingit patterns like people see on the totem poles. Everybody thinks that all Indians have teepees, totem poles and beaded eagle headdresses somewhere in the garage. The Apaches didn't have salmon or ravens. The Tlingit didn't have buffalo. Just goofy. I like Mrs. Warliss' carvings. All the eyes and noses were big. The lines were black, red and smooth. None of the carvings were the same. When we carved Mrs. Warliss let me rock. I didn't rock as much.

"Sorry for throwing the Shakespeare book at you." Daphne said during class when the third kid was home with a cold. I rocked faster and nodded.

"It's okay. I thought you would like it. Mom explained that you probably didn't understand." I kept rocking.

"It's just the other kids made fun of me after you wrote that story and put my name in as the princess."

"I'm going to be a famous crime novelist. I wrote a story about the ghost of Frank Reid and the construction site, but Mrs. Clements said to write something else because Mrs. Schumacher was mad."

"I'm sorry about your dad." she whispered.

"He didn't do anything. Someone was at the construction site shooting at the lights. I ran away. They shot at me. Dad was at home."

Daphne wrinkled her nose and frowned. "Mom said they thought your dad took you hunting and tried to make it look like an accident. They said he couldn't do it. Somehow he missed and hit your leg and tried to take you to Juneau to cover it up before the cops could find him. It was all over town. Mr. Schumacher spoke to the reporters and told them just a little bit of the story.

Mrs. Warliss walked by just as Daphne said that. She sighed and put down the chisel she picked off the shelf. "Daphne, Harry is a good guy. There's just a huge mix-up. What Harold needs right now is for people to see his dad as a good guy."

"But Mom says when he was younger he shot someone." Mrs. Warliss sat down and put her hands on the carving table like she was praying.

"Harry has had a rough go of things since high school. When he was young, everyone went to Juneau or Anchorage to look for work. Anyone that grew up in Skagway wanted to see the world and bust out in a big way. Well, the work in Anchorage put him around some rough characters. It's really hard work. It makes good money. All that hard work and money ends up going to a kid's head. Harry was at some party where they were playing cards. He was just a kid. He got cheated out of his pay in a crooked game. He was a hothead just like Mr. Schumacher. He confronted the guy. The guy jumped him, and they started fighting. The gun went off. It was an accident."

"My dad is a good guy."

"I know, Honey. So, Daphne, what Harold here needs the most is someone to carve with him. The rumors need to just be left alone. Make sense?" Daphne nodded. We had fifteen more minutes before the class was finished. It was dark at 3:03 in the afternoon that day. I was supposed to go home and vacuum. It was dark, but we were all used to it. I was just about finished. We picked up the tools. Putting the chisels away was easy. I was putting on my coat when the door busted open.

"ARREST HIM!!" Mr. Schumacher was red in the face and waving his arms. Sheriff Tate ran in behind him. Mr. Schumacher started running after me. I stumbled backward and fell. He grabbed me by the coat and picked me up. He shook me, and I screeched. All I remember from there was falling to the ground and crawling under the table and yelling some more. I wasn't the only one. Daphne stood there stunned. Mr. Schumacher was babbling and his face looked like a tomato. I covered my ears and whimpered. Sheriff Tate came between Mr. Schumacher and me under the table. Mrs. Warliss pushed Mr. Schumacher away from the table. In between grunts and shouts the adults looked like kids on a playground. Sheriff Tate had that look on his face. It's the look all the teachers get on their face when they try to calm me down during a fit. They don't know what to do.

"What's his problem?" Mrs. Warliss shouted.

"Construction site again." Sheriff Tate said. "Somebody cranked on the fire hydrant a block up the street. Even dug a small ditch. The construction site is the lowest part of the ground. Soaked, flooded and froze the whole thing in about six inches of ice. It's the Fourth of July all over again. Somebody lobbed a bunch of home-made bombs over the fence." Mrs. Warliss and Sheriff Tate made a human wall between me and Mr. Schumacher, waving their arms. He gave up. Mr. Schumacher stood their huffing and puffing. My mom came to the door and knelt down under the table to check on me.

"That retard is a menace! I'm not going to let this town stay locked in 1898 without any progress!" Mr. Schumacher was different shades of red. Mom ignored him. Sheriff Tate got him out of the recreation hall. Mom gave me a cough drop. Daphne and Mrs. Warliss stayed until I was better. I went home with Mom. She said I didn't have to vacuum.

"They think Dad shot me, Mom."

"I know, Honey."

"The ghost of Frank Reid has to help us."

"Somebody is trying. Just not sure they are going about it the right way."

Chapter 18

When I went back to school, Mrs. Clements was tired but glad to see me. She didn't leave me in the hallway. Daphne stopped by the special kid room to get me at lunch. She helped me get through the lunch line without people bothering me. Some of them ignored me by pointing and staring. That's not the definition of ignoring someone, but that's what they thought they were doing. When you ignore someone you don't point.

A couple of them tried to say "Hi, Rocky." I kind of waved and looked at the ground. Rudy was the only one who ignored me in a strange way. He acted like I was a vampire. He got a scared look on his face when he looked at me. Then he would get a mad look on his face. Once he punched a locker. He didn't have his wrestling jacket on. Just a normal coat like everyone else. The coach gave me stinky eyes when he walked by. It went like that for a couple of days.

Then a big kid bumped me hard with his shoulder. He snarled like Melvin used to back when I was in third grade. "Nice going, retard." Mark was a wrestler. He had his wrestling jacket on. He looked at the coach who was walking down the hallway. I just blinked at Mark. He had never talked to me before. "Rudy just quit the team because of you." I looked right and left. His breath smelled like hot dogs. I ran back to Mrs. Clements class, took out my notebook and started writing.

"Everything okay, Harold?" Mrs. Clements asked. I nodded, rocked and kept writing. "You know that it's music class right now." I nodded and kept writing. She could see from the way I was rocking that it was a safer bet to let me keep writing. Trying to get me to class when I was upset was a nightmare. That's what Mrs. Martinez said back when I was a Bluebird with all the little babies in first grade. I didn't understand why Rudy would quit the team. He was going to be a state champion. Dad said he had the best of both worlds for a wrestler. He was as strong as a bear and quick as a fox. Usually you get one or the other. Dad said Mr. Schumacher only had the strong as a bear part. I pictured Rudy wrestling bears in the forest. I didn't know why he quit. The rest of the day went fine. Mom let me go to bed early after dinner. The next day Daphne ran up to me as I was walking to school. She lived one street over. This was out of her way.

"Watch yourself today, Rocky. Rudy quit the team because of what his dad did to you. The coach is really mad."

"I didn't do anything. I didn't tell him to quit the team."

Daphne started talking really fast. "My mom says the whole town is buzzing. Mr. Feeney from the hardware store has Rudy buying spray paint on his security camera. He said he could tell it was Rudy because of the letterman's jacket. Whoever messed up the construction site this time used bright orange all over the posts. Mr. Richardson, the chemistry teacher said some chemical was missing from the supply closet. Rudy was a teacher's aide for chemistry. Mr. Richardson said they just finished a unit on what makes reactions go fast or slow."

"What does that matter?" I asked.

"That's what makes explosions. It's when chemical reactions go really, really, fast." Daphne said.

"But how do you know all of this?"

"My mom works the lunch shift at the diner. Sheriff Tate has had to order his lunch delivered on account of all the state police involved in the case. Mom said the whole station is going nuts right now. It doesn't look good for Rudy."

"Rudy is my friend. He wouldn't do anything bad."

"Well not everybody believes you now. Sheriff Tate came and took Rudy to jail. Make sure to write it down in your notebook. There might be some clues somewhere to help Rudy. I'll come by and help you at lunch." We were at the steps of the school. Daphne waved goodbye. I wish I could give her the works of Shakespeare like a normal person.

Mrs. Clements smiled at me when I came into the room. She looked both ways down the hallway before closing the door. "Everything okay, Harold?" I nodded. I took three steps forward and one to the right. That's where my coat hook was. They didn't put names above our hooks anymore, but everyone knew that was my coat hook. There was a coat on the hook. Mom said it didn't matter. I could find a new coat hook. I heard the birds start to flap in my head. I dumped the coat on the ground and put my coat on my coat hook.

"Hey! That's my coat. Pick it up!" Daniel was getting out of his desk. Mrs. Clements was already at her desk.

I looked at the ground. "It's my coat hook."

"Geez! You can't just dump somebody's coat. It's not your lucky coat hook. Just pick somewhere else!"

"That's where I always put my coat." I walked away. Daniel dumped my coat and put his back on the hook. Mom told me not to get in trouble. Mom told me to come up with a plan B. I didn't want a plan B. I just wanted to put my coat on my hook. I swung my backpack at Daniel. He fell into the desk with a crash. Mrs. Clements turned around and looked at Daniel. She looked at me. She wasn't smiling at me. I ended up in the hallway with my backpack. I had my notebook. I was in the hallway for a long time that day. Daphne came by and picked me up for lunch.

"We have to hide you, Rocky." She grabbed my hand. She pulled. She wanted me to run.

"Why do I have to hide?"

"Mr. Schumacher hired some of the wrestlers to pound you. Mark says they're going to send a message to the rabble-rousers."

"A message?"

"They want to make you confess to making the construction site blow up. They want to make it so Rudy gets out of jail. Mom said the jail is buzzing with all sorts of reporters and cops. They all want to get you."

"I can't hide. I rock. Then I yell. Slow down." We were running down the hall. Daphne was looking backward. We heard the cafeteria door bang open and Mark talking to his friends.

"In here!" She didn't ask. She shoved me into Mr. Richardson's empty chemistry classroom. "Duck!" I went under the lab table like she said. Bunches of voices and mumbling footsteps stomped through the hall.

"But I didn't do anything," I whispered.

"I already got your coat. Here. Put this on." Daphne was ignoring me.

"That's no big deal. We all put on our coat in the cafeteria before lunch. It's lunch time. It's cold."

"I couldn't take a chance you'd forget your coat. Hurry. Mom is behind the building. Aunt Edna came up with the plan. Your mom will meet us at the train station."

"We're taking the train?"

"I don't know. I just know Mom told me to get you here during lunch. Hurry!" There were more mumbling steps from other people in the hallway. They were getting louder. We snuck out the side door and into the powder blue Buick LeSabre warming up behind the school. "Got him, Mom." Daphne said. Daphne's mom, Mrs. Tyler gave me a syrup smile that people give to Special Ed kids when they don't know what to do. Daphne looked like her mom. Her mom was just a fluffier version of Daphne with a couple of wrinkles. My mom was soft like that. Mrs. Greene didn't eat as much as Mom. She was skinnier than both of them.

"Sorry for all the confusion, Harold. We had to do something fast before they came to the school." Mrs. Tyler said.

"What do they want?" I asked.

"You. Somehow, Mr. Schumacher has convinced child services to come sooner than expected. They visited this morning."

"Natalie is sick. She was home sick today."

"Well, Natalie was trying to be a good girl and help your mother out with the dishes. The case worker asked all sorts of questions and Natalie got scared. She made Natalie get in the car with her and then they were coming to the school to get you next."

"But Mom was at work. We cleaned the house. They weren't supposed to come so soon."

Daphne blurted, "Mom, on top of that the wrestling team was waiting in the lunch room to pound on Rocky."

"What?"

"Susan told me that they've been doing different things for Mr. Schumacher. They are really mad that Rudy quit the team. They blame Rocky. They got really mad when Sheriff Tate came this morning and picked Rudy up straight out of Algebra. It's all over school. The wrestlers are sure Rocky did it. They don't think Rudy would be stupid enough to throw away the state championship."

"Why did Sheriff Tate go after him?"

"We all watched from the window. Sheriff Tate took Rudy out to his truck. He waved around spray paint cans and the monkey wrench big enough to loosen the fire hydrant in the back of his pick-up. Rudy looked at the ground and then the Sheriff shoved Rudy in the back of the squad car. Then he tossed the spray cans and wrench in his trunk."

"That doesn't help his situation." Mrs. Tyler said.

"They also found the chemical he used to make the bombs." Daphne continued.

"School rumors must be really spinning today. What kind?"

"No, it's true! Something or other aluminum chloride. Rudy was a really good chemistry student. Sheriff Tate came into the chemistry and kept asking the teacher questions." Daphne was still talking really fast.

"It still doesn't make sense. Why are they so upset at Rocky?" Mrs. Tyler kept asking.

"Mr. Schumacher has the whole school thinking Rocky is some kind of lunatic. They don't believe it." Daphne said.

Mrs. Tyler looked in the rear view mirror. "Well the diner is spinning like a tornado with gossip too. Skagway is too small for a fly to land in bear poop for too long without everybody knowing it. It doesn't help that Rudy pled guilty to the entire thing. He wants to stay in jail. He wants a lawyer. Mr. Schumacher says he's gone insane. He wants to take the hospital and get him check out. He even ordered a helicopter from Juneau. There are officials here from HVI. They want to try and figure out what is happening to the construction site." Daphne's mom was looking around every corner. They told me to lie down in the back seat under the blanket.

"Why would Rudy want to stay in jail?" I asked.

"He even told Sheriff Tate that if he gets to stay in jail he has more information on the construction site problems. Ralph— Mr. Schumacher is having a conniption." She turned into the back entrance of the Skagway Mercantile building. She took me and Daphne into one of the back rooms where they store boxes and boxes of t-shirts. "Now, don't worry about a thing. Aunt Edna is down at the station with your mom, Harold."

"His name is Rocky." Daphne said.

"We don't have time for that now, Daphne. Now listen. Just stay put. Aunt Edna is going to come get you when it gets dark. That should only be about an hour. You can stay with her tonight. You'll have to lay low a couple of days until Monica and her lawyer can come up on the weekend with the ferry.

"Umm—." I said.

"Yes, Harold?"

"Never mind. I'll just write in my notebook."

"You do that." She closed the door. It was warm and quiet.

"Daphne do you know what time it is?" I asked. She dug out her phone and looked at the time.

"It's 1:37."

I wrote 1:37 at the top of the page. Mom told me to write down the time when my schedule wasn't working out like normal. This wasn't normal.

Chapter 19

It was a cold, dark night. I could see my breath in the moonlight. Aunt Edna waited until the HVI hot shots were in their hotel rooms. We were walking to her house in the dark. She waited to come get me until Mr. Schumacher had gone to dinner with them and then disappeared into the back of his shop. Mr. Feeney was keeping an eye on him.

"We should be okay. I made a loud announcement in the police station that I was staying across the street with Mrs. Sydney. I didn't want them to spy on my house and see you here. You were right about the ghost of Frank Reid." Aunt Edna said. She said if we walked in the shadows it would look less suspicious than using her car. Nobody much drives around at night. She didn't want to give Sheriff Tate a reason to have to stop her. "He's been leaving notes on Ralph's car all week. Ralph is pacing up and down everywhere. He keeps looking over his shoulder. The notes keep telling Mr. Schumacher to clean up his act or suffer the fate of Soapy Smith. Mr. Feeney says he's pretty rattled. Not sure I believe in the phantom haunting thing yet. Just hope the ghost doesn't go too far. A cornered bear is more dangerous than one on the run." She said. I yawned.

"Can I get something to eat?" My hands were cold.

"Why of course you can. We're almost there." Mrs. Tyler said, "You've been such a trooper."

"What happened to Natalie?" I asked.

"Well since they can't get out of Skagway until morning the social worker is keeping Natalie with her. She rented an extra hotel room so Natalie would have a place to stay. Poor thing is scared out of her wits. Your mother is beside herself."

"You can't sit beside yourself. That would mean there are two of you." I said.

"I guess you are right. She is very upset." Aunt Edna's house smelled like cookies. "I told you I'd make you some cookies. Why don't you sit down and eat some clam chowder. Then you can have some cookies. I made it fresh yesterday but I can't eat it all by myself." Aunt Edna's clam chowder was really thick. It tasted great. Mom didn't care for clams so we usually had something else in our chowder. Aunt Edna gave me some hot cocoa. Usually Mom would tell me to limit my sweets but Aunt Edna didn't know. I felt sleepy. Aunt Edna had a spare bedroom near the back door next to the utility room. She had me brush my teeth and get under the covers while she did the dishes. After finished my teeth and crawled in bed I snagged my notebook. Aunt Edna tapped on the door. It creaked when it opened. I was writing. "You try to get some sleep, now. It's a bit drafty in here but you it should be better than the mercantile storage closet." Aunt Edna smiled. I put my notebook back into my backpack. She didn't have to tuck me in but I didn't argue. She was an old lady. They thought everyone was a little baby. She was nice. I nodded when she said, "Good Night," and she clicked off the light. I didn't tell her I'd left all my clothes and shoes on. Mom didn't fight me on getting all the way ready for bed when I had a bad day. If I had just a little bit of a bad day then my schedule for getting ready helped calm me down. This was a big bad day. My clothes were still on. The moonlight turned the whole room blue. I stared at the giant 'X's up on the wall made by the shadow from the checkerboard window. I must have drifted off. Mrs. Edna shook me awake.

"Harold, Harold, Honey get up." Aunt Edna was panicking. Her hair was around her shoulders. Not like a tight frosted donut bun she always wore. She had on a flowery house coat. She squinted. "Hurry, Honey. We need to go."

"Is it morning?"

"No, Honey. Now grab your backpack. We need to go out the back."

"What's that glow?" I asked.

"I'll let you know as soon as we get out." Aunt Edna tried not to push me but she was in a hurry. I glanced over my shoulder and noticed why. Flames were licking the corner of the house. Fire was crawling across the ceiling and coming our way. Her house was on fire. The cold air smacked my face as we went into the back yard. "This way." Aunt Edna said. I told them I was with Mrs. Sydney. We need to go around the block and act surprised." She was very serious. Her eyes were tired.

"Shouldn't we get your furniture out?"

"No time for that. Hopefully the firemen will put it out soon." There were shouts. Neighbors dressed and half-dressed all emptied out of their houses. Some of the men were running to get hoses. Aunt Edna shuffled us around the block and then put me near the back, behind a tree. "Now you stay here." I watched the flames eat up her house. I stayed behind the tree. People kept shouting. Mom ran up to Aunt Edna and whispered something in her ear. I wanted to wave but Sheriff Tate was there. Aunt Edna glanced at me once and held her finger to her lips so I would be quiet. Mom didn't see me. The shadows of the crowd bounced off of the fire truck. Mr. Feeney jumped off the truck and started ordering the other guys to hook up the hoses. Everybody in Skagway does two or three jobs. Mr. Schumacher was a fireman and the mayor besides owning his beef jerky gift shop. Mr. Schumacher wasn't there.

The house burned and burned. People stayed out of the way. Firemen in their bathrobes yelled. Mr. Schumacher came late. He stared at the flames like he was watching TV. I didn't know what to do. "Coming to see your handiwork?" Somebody mumbled at the back of his head. He didn't turn around. He didn't help put the fire out. "You crossed the line, Ralph. First your boy goes bonkers and now you." He didn't turn around. People were angry. Mr. Schumacher turned his back and stomped down the dark street. Mr. Feeney ignored him the whole time. The crowd mumbled quite a bit. Aunt Edna picked up Mr. Schumacher's faraway look off of the street and put it on her face. She also picked up a piece of paper. She knew something just like Mr. Schumacher knew something. She couldn't stomp down the street. She had to sit in the middle of the town in her pajamas. I felt bad for her.

"Hey. *Psst!*" It was Daphne. "You need to come with us." Her mom's Buick was parked two blocks away. The air was still cool and clear. The moon didn't leave us many shadows. I liked looking at the blue grass on the ground. The gravel crunched under my feet. It was one of those times when life punches you so hard in the gut you remember everything. Even what isn't important. Daphne tried to make me feel better. "Grandma lives behind the café. It makes it easier to open for the old fisherman. They are always leaving at dark thirty in the morning."

"I don't understand dark thirty." I wrote down PIDU 14. We got in the car. It was too dark for me to duck down. They let me sit up and watch the glow of the fire.

Daphne was watching too. Mrs. Tyler said, "It means really early in the morning. I can't believe they went this far. This is out of control." We got in the house and closed the door. Her mom had her hair in curlers. She was had a jacket over some sweats. Only Aunt Edna wore her pajamas outside. Daphne's house was smaller than Aunt Edna's. They set up an old cot in the living room. It was for me. I wanted to stay awake but everything was just too much for me. My clothes smelled like smoke. Usually I would throw a fit. I was too tired. It didn't take long for me to fall asleep. I had dreams and nightmares of Frank Reid chasing me through the burning house. Then I had dreams that I was in jail with Dad and they wouldn't let me have my notebooks even though it held clues. Colors and shouts all swirled around in my head. I don't remember much else.

"Hey, you okay?" Daphne's mom was nudging me awake. Sunlight was coming in the window." I screamed. I didn't know where I was. "It's okay. I'm Daphne's mom, Mrs. Tyler. Remember? Remember the fire last night?" I was rocking. I snatched my notebook and started writing.

"What time is it?"

"Well, I guess it's—."

"I need the time."

"It's around 10 o'clock."

"That's not the time. I need the *time!*" I was really agitated. I was trying to keep the bees out of my head all on my own without my mom's help this time. It was torture. Daphne's mom hurried to the kitchen and looked at her microwave.

"It says here that it's 9:53." I wrote it in my book. I was really agitated.

"I take my pill at 7:00. I take my pill at 7:00." The bees were buzzing and I couldn't write enough to make them slow down.

"Oh, land's sake, I forgot. I felt so bad for you I didn't want to wake you." Mrs. Tyler ran into their kitchenette and came back with a pill and some water. "I take my pill at 7:00. I take my pill at 7:00." Daphne's grandmother walked in. She was adjusting her apron. I didn't want to panic. I picked up my notebook and started to write but I was rocking really bad.

"Why don't you come help me wash some dishes? I need someone who can stack lots and lots of dishes in one place. "Can you rock and stack at the same time? Can you do that?" I nodded. I put my notebook in my backpack. "Oh, you smell like you've been standing in a chimney. Don't you have some of Corey's old clothes that could fit?" Grandma Tyler was taller than Aunt Edna. She was wearing a waitress outfit and some white shoes. She didn't mind my rocking. She sat on the sofa across from my cot. Grandma Tyler smiled and folded her hands in front of her. "Can you help me like you help your mom?" She had jiggly arms like my mom.

I kept rocking. "I think so. I take my medicine at 7:00."

"I understand, perfectly. We stop breakfast service at 11:00. You can't go serving eggs and bacon at 11:30. Just wouldn't be right." She gave me a wink. I kept rocking and smiled. Mrs. Tyler came out with a rugby shirt and some jeans. The jeans didn't fit but she found some old sweatpants that worked. I hiked them up with my wrist, grabbed my backpack and followed Grandma Tyler. She had one of the bubble rumps that made the apron strings bounce up and down.

"Keep him out of sight." Mrs. Tyler said. She didn't have a bubble rump. She wore sweats quite a bit. I couldn't tell if she worked in the café.

"Oh, course. We wouldn't want the ghost of Frank Reid to have all the fun." She winked at me again. "The café is all a buzz. I haven't had this much business in the wintertime since the governor did the ribbon cutting. Those HVI types sure are tight MMWLMSTW."

"Language, Mildred." Mrs. Tyler scolded.

"Oh, loosen up. You're enjoying this spy game too much."

"Tell me you aren't enjoying sticking it to Ralph."

"Well we're not supposed to like it so much. Sets a bad example. Huh, Champ." Grandma Tyler winked again. She went out the door and I followed her.

"My name is Rocky."

"Of course it is." We walked to the kitchen. It was noisy and I winced when I first got there. Steam came up from fried eggs and the cook was yelling something at the skinny guy carrying the tub of dishes. He was one of the Filipino guys that stayed year round. Aunt Edna said he didn't talk much. Grandma Tyler set me up in front of the dishwasher. It was easy stacking the dishes. I liked doing the job. It kept my hands busy and nobody cared if I rocked. It was a little too loud for me with the dishes clanking and Grandma Tyler yelling things back and forth at Jerry, the cook. He mumbled to himself quite a bit about working as a chef in the big leagues. I finally asked Grandma Tyler if she had earmuffs. She was confused. "Try sticking pieces of napkins in your ears. Just don't shove them so far down I have to helicopter you to Juneau. That would blow your cover for sure."

At some point Grandma Tyler came and made me hang up my apron. She gave me a hamburger and fries with extra ketchup. I don't know how she knew I liked extra ketchup. I took it across the little yard behind the café and into the house. School was out and Daphne was dumping her backpack on the table before she went to work. She helped out in the café too, cleaning up. I guess I was doing her job but she didn't seem to mind.

"I almost burst trying not to tell anybody where you were! You'd go nuts at what kids are saying." I munched on a French fry and pulled out my notebook. I was careful not to spill ketchup. "One girl thinks that the Russians jewelry store owners have mob ties. She said they put you on ice because you screwed up the construction site so much. It didn't help that the HVI guys *and* state cops came down and pulled Mrs. Clements out of class *three times*."

Mrs. Daphne folded somebody's underwear and put it on one of the piles on the couch. "Now Daphne, don't scare Rocky. He's been holding up pretty well."

"What else are they saying?" I asked. I ignored the underwear. Somebody had bigger brown streaks than I do.

"That's where it gets *really* strange. Turns out the Mark and Alex were out sick today. Coach Clark was pulled out by the state police. He left in the back of their car in the middle of the school day. All the wrestlers were absent, or walking around with their heads down. There is going to be an emergency city council meeting on Saturday night. It was going to be tonight but the whole town is trying to help Aunt Edna take care of what is left of her house. Rudy is still in jail and Mr. Schumacher is following the HVI people around everywhere but he isn't talking. The cops are absolutely *bonkers* about not being able to find you. The social worker is calling up every agency she can find. Your mom is a queen, now. She has the whole town on her side. The social worker is going crazy. I about burst not telling anybody."

"Well you can't burst. People don't burst. Only bubbles and balloons." I said. Daphne giggled. I reached in my backpack for one of my old notebooks. I wanted to check out what I had written before.

"Notebook 113 is missing!" I scrambled and dumped my backpack. I was rocking and moaning."

"Well we'll just get you another notebook."

"We can't! It had all sorts of times and information in it. Dad told me to keep my notebooks. I was finishing it at Aunt Edna's before I fell asleep."

"Well I'm sure it's long gone by now with the fire, Dear." Mrs. Tyler gave me a sad look. I knew I had to be quiet now. I knew that it was too important to explain. Even if it was impossible I had to go try and see if it was there. I'm not stupid. I remember important things. That notebook could help Rudy and Dad. I had to try. I had a plan. I wouldn't screw it up like the time I got shot. I just couldn't tell them where I was going. I had to be like Mickey Spillane. I had to try and go back to Aunt Edna's house and look.

Chapter 20

So much for being Mickey Spillane. He never fell through the floor of a building he was investigating. Now everyone was going to get mad again. I didn't mean for it to happen. I planned it all out. I got a dark coat from the hallway. I waited until it was midnight. I wrote it down in my notebook. I stayed out of the moonlight when I walked to Aunt Edna's house. It made me feel horrible. Her house looked like a Jack-O-Lantern somebody smashed at Halloween. They had pulled most of the furniture out of the way and all there was a floor with about half a corner left. The roof looked like a top of the Jack-O-Lantern, tilted, smashed and jagged. I stayed out of the moonlight and walked to the back. I remembered the room was next to the utility room. There was charred cylinder. It must have been the hot water heater the small steps up to the kitchen were still there. The roof was propped up by the kitchenette top in that one area. I crawled underneath to see if I could get to where the room was.

That's when the floor collapsed under me. I fell into the crawl space under the house with a loud bang. Pieces of the floor, duct and rocks fell in with me letting the moonlight cut through parts of the room to where I was sitting. The roof groaned like it wanted to keep falling. The pile of dust and cobwebs covered my face. I yelled at first. Luckily I had a flashlight. I looked around. I'm not stupid. I was scared but I wasn't stupid. I turned off the light so nobody could find me. I had to wait. After all Aunt Edna lived in Frank Reid's house. His ghost would have to know I was there. He would have to let somebody know I was there. I crawled to a place where the moonlight was shining like its own flashlight. That way I could keep writing. I would just keep writing and ignore the cold. I was sure Frank Reid would tell my mom or Aunt Edna. My backpack was dusty. I pulled it off and started to unzip the back. I scanned where I was so I could have a back rest.

That's when I found it. Part of the foundation of the house stuck out like a chimney. The problem was that the utility room where I fell into the crawl space was at the south end of the house. I knew the chimney was at the north end of the house. There was no reason for the foundation to stick out. Dad showed me that moss grows on the north. He used Aunt Edna's chimney while all of the women were cooking and chattering. When I fell into the hole a piece of the roof did too. This wasn't the north part of the roof next to the chimney. The moss was on the wrong side. It was cold and creepy like squishy carpet. I could also see more cobwebs.

That wasn't the only thing. When the roof fell, it cracked open this fake chimney next to me like a boiled egg. My flashlight showed me an old pocket watch, some cuff links and a crunched metal box about the size of a lunch pail. It had faded letters I couldn't quite make out. It had to be important. I got all tingly like the day I found a ten dollar bill by the back door of our house in Juneau when I was six. I looked through a few more things and then shut my light off. I put the things in my backpack and scooted to a safer place in the crawl space next to the wall. I used the moonlight shining through a crack in the floor to write in my notebook and clicked off the light. Someday I would quit falling through the floor and getting shot out. That would give me time to become a famous crime novelist. My toes were starting to talk to me about the cold. Kind of the opposite of a stranger trying to grab my hand. I listened to my body quite a bit. It was getting harder to write in my notebook. There was gravel crunching and voices about so I shoved the contents of the fake chimney deeper into my backpack, zipped it up and listened.

"Rocky!" Someone was doing that half yell half whisper thing. There was another voice.

"Harold!" They were older. One was a woman. I heard the gravel crunching faster and faster under their feet. "Oh, I hope he's not hurt, Nick."

"Thanks for coming Mr. Feeney." They were all whisper yelling. The last voice was younger.

"Let's just hope he wasn't dumb enough to try and go into what is left of that house. I can't guarantee the structure is stable. Parts of it might even still be burning." That's when I knew it was Daphne and Mrs. Tyler. I knew Frank Reid would send someone to find me.

"Over here!" It was my turn to whisper-yell. I kind of just yelled. I flashed my flash light on and off to get their attention. The gravel crunched even faster.

"Stand back. That roof could collapse all the way. Are you hurt?" Mr. Feeney said.

"No. I just fell in when the floor collapsed. I'm in the crawl space."

"Just a minute." There were fading footsteps.

"Harold, what were you thinking?" Mrs. Tyler wasn't all the way whispering. "You terrified me!"

"I just wanted to find my notebook. It's important."

"Did you find it?" Daphne asked.

"Something even better." I said.

"What is it?"

"I can't tell, yet. I need to talk to Aunt Edna and Mrs. Greene." I was tired of adults getting in the way. Mr. Feeney was nice but I didn't know who to trust. A light from where I fell through the floor started bouncing around. I was sitting about six feet from where I fell in. I could see dust in the moonlight.

More footsteps. "Back away from the hole a minute." There was a crunch. An ax split some wood around the hole. I crouched along one wall while the hole got bigger and bigger. I wasn't all the way under the roof. It was by the kitchen. The roof groaned again but seemed like it wanted to go stay in place. A ladder slid carefully into place in the bigger hole. "OK, now climb out slowly. Careful not to touch the roof." I hopped on the bottom rung as fast as I could and popped out like a rabbit.

"That wasn't smart." Mr. Feeney was winding up for a lecture.

"Not now, Nick. People are going to be wondering about the chopping and the roof." Mrs. Tyler was looking over her shoulder. "Give him the lecture later." She hissed.

I was cold and covered in dirt. "I didn't mean to scare you. I just had an idea, like the night I visited the construction site to talk to Frank Reid's ghost."

"Construction site?" Did you get a look at the vandal?" Mr. Feeney whispered.

"Only once, but it was dark. The second time was when someone shot me."

"Let's go." Mrs. Tyler hissed again, waving me to the alley where her car was parked.

"You didn't get shot by your dad in a hunting accident?" Mr. Feeney blurted, sounding confused.

Mrs. Tyler gently pushed my head down so I wouldn't bump it on the car door. "I'll let you know what he says, Nick. I just saw Mrs. Collins' back porch light go on." We all piled in her car. A curtain moved in the window. Mr. Feeney took off down the road in his truck the opposite way. I watched out the back window to see if Mrs. Collins had turned off her light.

"You stink." Daphne said. "You're sure your Dad didn't shoot you? That's what everybody thinks.

"My dad didn't shoot me. My dad didn't mess up the construction site. He's in jail. He didn't magically get out just to flood the lumber with water. My dad was in the back of the house with my mom the night I got shot."

"No more questions, Daphne. We're just glad you're safe, Harold." Mrs. Tyler said.

"His name is Rocky. He's going to be a famous crime novelist." I couldn't see much of her face but I think she smiled. We got back to Daphne's house and Mrs. Tyler made me take a bath. The house was warm. I promised not to run away any more. It was nice to be warm again.

The next three days were quiet. Mrs. Tyler remembered to give my pill at 7:00 am. Grandma Tyler let me wash dishes as much as I wanted. It was nice to be helpful. The noise would get to me and I stuck pieces of napkins in my ears. My mom stopped by late on the third day and visited me in the kitchen. She hugged me way too tight like I was a baby but I didn't say anything. I went back to counting and organizing the plates that were coming out of the washing machine. The steam almost burned my face but I didn't say anything. I wasn't a baby.

"I hear you have some big secret in your backpack." Mom said. I nodded. "Well it turns out I have a secret too. Want to hear it?"

I shook my head no. "Then it won't be a secret. I need to work, here, Mom. I don't want Sheriff Tate to catch me and take me to autism jail." Mom kissed my forehead. My forehead was sweaty.

"You're right, Detective. We don't want you to go to autism jail. Just a little while longer and we'll be home free."

"I won't be free of autism. It's not exactly like a gunshot but it's a little like jail."

"Why do you say that, Detective?"

"You can escape jail. You can't escape autism."

"Oh, escaping is overrated. I can't escape these floppy arms." She jiggled the fat above her elbow.

"Your floppy arms are fine. That's what makes you a mom."

"Well, Detective, then your autism is fine. That's what makes you Harold Reginald Blackbear Jones III."

"Call me Rocky."

"Harold. You'll always be Harold to your mother."

"Mickey Spillane had a cool name. I'm going to be a famous crime novelist and go by the name Rocky."

"I'm sure you will, Harold. But I'm your mother. I changed your diapers, so—."

"Mom!" I scowled, looking behind me. The cook was smiling. "Don't embarrass me. I'm not a baby!"

"Well, I'll be going then Detective. I'll let you get back to solving your crime."

I finished my job and Mrs. Tyler let me go back to the house. I pulled out my notebook and started writing. It turned out I had plenty to write about just by listening to people talk while I stood by the dishwasher all day. For instance, Rudy won the argument about where to stay. He stayed in jail. He was getting visits from some wrestlers. The ghost of Frank Reid was picking on Mr. Schumacher. Frank was leaving notes all over his truck and gift store. One day he even let the air out of two of his tires. Grandma Tyler said the whole town was chuckling when Mr. Schumacher started yelling at the sky in the middle of Main Street.

He wasn't happy that HVI requested a special state mediator to run the city council on Saturday. They said that with Rudy in jail it looked bad to have Mr. Schumacher talk for them. Nobody in town was talking to the reporters other than to say they were all looking for me day and night. The social worker told them I was kidnapped by the vandals. The state police hot shots were not very nice. They kept ordering Sheriff Tate around. The longer I was gone the worse it looked for the social worker and the state. Aunt Edna told the paper that the social worker was wrong and she hoped Mom filed a complaint.

I was glad when Mrs. Greene got there with her lawyer. That's when Mom and I met with them at Daphne's house. Mom gave them what she found out. I gave Mrs. Greene the box and what I found in the chimney. She put her hand to her mouth like she was going to cry. She hugged me. Even though it made my arm scream a little I didn't mind. Her lawyer smiled. We were all set for city council.

Chapter 21

"Do you swear to tell the truth, the whole truth and nothing but the truth, so help you God?" Everyone nodded with their right hand up. "I now commission each testimony in this hearing to be at risk of perjury according to the laws of the State of Alaska." Judge Stanley said he wasn't acting like a real judge in a court case but he sure looked like one. It was supposed to be a city council meeting but everything changed when they couldn't find me and the state police were there. Judge Stanley stared down his long nose and over his glasses a bit. He had silver hair slicked back and he frowned like he just finished eating lemons for lunch. We all sat down. "Now understand that this is simply a mediation hearing. We will take testimonies. Counselors will simply listen. There will be no formal cross examination. We are mostly here to hear the testimonies of various parties so that future decisions can be made in the best interest of Harold. We also want to determine what future decisions need to be made between HVI and Skagway. In either case, any criminal behavior would be taken into account at a later date if anything should arise from the testimony." I had to write as fast as I could to get it all in my notebook. I was rocking. Mom tried to pat my knee three times but she gave up. I kept writing. She just made sure I had a spare pen in case something happened to this one. She knew writing was the key to keeping me in the room and calmed down. Mr. Cooper's breath smelled like tobacco and fish. He was sitting behind me.

They snuck me in the door at the last minute. We were sitting in the back row. The social worker saw me and turned red in the face. Mom ignored her. Natalie waved. I waved back. Sheriff Tate explained to the judge at the last minute why I was hiding in town and he allowed it until after the hearing. The crowd murmured and everyone started looking at me. They were murmuring like the bees were outside my head. Judge banged his gavel. The bees stopped. I kept writing. "The State calls Ralph Schumacher to the stand." Mr. Schumacher frowned just like the judge. His frown looked more like he wanted to punch someone in the face. Mr. Schumacher was sitting in the front row. It didn't take him long to sit next to the microphone. "Mr. Schumacher, please explain your role with HVI and how it relates to the vandalism. From your perspective how are Harold Reginald Blackbear Jr. and Harold Reginald Blackbear III connected to this situation?"

Mr. Schumacher frowned. "As the mayor of Skagway I was on a financial diplomatic mission. HVI came up with a proposal to improve the lives of us all. I was the liaison between the company and the town. We have a deal. People in the town are going to get new homes in Dyea while HVI builds a state of the art hotel here near the dock. We were going to have Main street professionally restored. Parts of it were going to be replicated from period photos down to the finest detail. Then that kid and his old man started getting in the way. They started hiring lawyers and messing with the construction site."

"You do realize your own son has confessed to the vandalism, Mr. Schumacher." Judge Stanley said.

"My son is under a great deal of pressure. It's not easy being in line to win the state championship. I believe that he is confused."

"Do you have anything else to add to your testimony?"

"Yes. I think that this entire misunderstanding is due to a couple of disgruntled citizens. Monica Greene is upset because she wants more control of her Aunt Edna's estate. Harry has always led a troubled and bitter life since he was disqualified from wrestling for state back when we were in high school. Wrestling was all he had. I think he is jealous of me winning the championship. He's really off his rocker. I feared for his family. I have it on good authority that he took his autistic son into the forest to pretend he had a hunting accident. That's how Harold was shot." People in the crowd were muttering. The bees in the room started buzzing again. Judge Stanley looked over his glasses to make the people be quiet. I wish I had a Judge Stanley in my head when the bees start buzzing.

"And who is this authority?"

"I can't answer that. It was told to me in confidence." The crowd muttered again. The judge looked at them again.

"Do you have final words to add?"

"Only that I think HVI is a great company and bending over backwards for Skagway. We really need to put this behind us and move forward with the project. Skagway will be the crown jewel of the cruise circuit." It was quieter but there was a little muttering.

"That will be all." We all waited while Mr. Schumacher got back to his seat. "Sheriff Tate, will you please take the stand?" Sheriff Tate was right next to the judge. He sat down next to the microphone and read from his police notes about all the vandalism. He told the judge about the first time someone pulled up the surveyor stakes. He told the judge about when they blew up the lumber. He told the judge about when they shot the camera and allegedly shot me. He told the judge about the fourth time when it was flooded. He also told Judge Stanley about how Rudy confessed to the entire thing and wanted to stay in jail instead of go to the hospital. Rudy said he did the entire thing. I know he had help but I just kept writing.

"Do you have anything else to add, Sheriff?"

"Rudy seems really upset about something he's not saying. He says he is through with his dad fixing things. He said Rocky would understand. His dad is handy with carpentry so I didn't understand what he meant. Rudy says he wants a lawyer. He not only confessed to the vandalism he apologized to HVI and said he would work it off if they would let him. He did ask to see Monica Greene this morning. I allowed the visit. She will explain later." The crowd muttered again but Judge Stanley didn't have to look over his glasses. Sheriff Tate stepped down.

"The next to testify is Lois Jones." Mom squeezed my shoulder. I kept rocking and writing. She borrowed a nice dress from Mrs. Tyler. Mom looked nice. She looked nervous. "Mrs. Jones, would you please explain your perspective around these events in question." Mom cleared her throat. She looked at her lap and smoothed her skirt with her hands.

"My son, Harold, is autistic, your Honor. To think that he had something to do with the vandalism has been cruel. I got a visit from the state and the social worker while he was recovering in Juneau from being shot. The night the video surveillance was shot he was down at the construction site. My husband and I were in the bedroom arguing about something. Everyone argues. That's not a crime. We didn't know he was down there. Harold has never run off before.

We know what people have been saying around here for years, but my husband Harry, really turned over a new leaf when his mother died. He promised her he would change and he has done a great job. He really has. It was making me feel sad that they town didn't know that."

"Mrs. Jones, please stick to the details of the shooting." Judge Stanley said. Mom nodded and looked down at her hands.

"After Harold was shot in the leg he came home and gave us a flashlight because the shots blew the transformer and killed the power around town. He ran right past us and went in his room and it was dark so we didn't see his leg right away. He wrapped his leg and stuck it in the air by leaning it on his bed."

"Are you telling me that Harold was shot and didn't even notice?" Judge Stanley didn't look up. He was taking some notes.

"He doesn't process things the same way. He noticed something happened. But for Harold a train wreck is the same thing as a tea cup hitting the ground. He doesn't filter things the same way we do as one thing being important than another. He may have thought being shot was just a scratch that hurt from something he bumped in the dark. He did what he thought he was supposed to do and then went back to writing in his notebook. That's what he always does. He was most focused on me not being there to brush his teeth exactly on schedule."

"And how did you proceed once you discovered your son had been shot in the leg, Mrs. Jones." Judge Stanley's voice was low and crunchy like a truck backing over gravel.

"When we found him and we rushed him into Dave to get the bullet out since we don't have a doctor here in town. Dave did what he could and told us to take him to Juneau the next day to get it checked out. Somebody wrote some story in the paper and the next thing we knew Harry was arrested.

We waited and waited for Harry to serve his time or get his lawyer to do what was right. Something finally broke in the case and they said Harry was coming home." Mom looked down at her hands again. "He was just about to get out but there was a paper-work problem. Our lawyer said to be patient. While we were waiting the letter from the social worker came telling me they were going to take my kids away from me." Mom was starting to cry. Sheriff Tate handed her some tissue. She kept talking after a bit. "We came back to Skagway, enrolled Harold and Natalie in school. I got some part time jobs to make ends meet. The next thing I knew that lady has Natalie locked up and Harold disappeared. I was so afraid. Things have been happening all over town. Someone tore down Aunt Edna's car port. Mrs. Sydney's had her fence smashed in. When I asked Monica, she said that not everyone had quick-deeded their property over to Mr. Schumacher." People were muttering quite a bit now. "Mr. Schumacher made it sound like we were all on board. There were a few hold outs." It was the HVI men who were whispering now. Mr. Schumacher glared at my mom.

"In your opinion, who are these people holding out, Mrs. Jones?"

"I don't know them all. Aunt Edna was the biggest hold out."

"But the hotel wasn't going to come close to Aunt Edna's house. Why did she care?"

"Lawrence Henderson, Monica Greene and Aunt Edna understand that better than I do, your Honor. All I know is that I'm a good mother and the social worker has locked away my daughter because she listened to a bunch of rumors. Somebody else shot my son that night. He struggles with autism and people around here are doing a great job helping us raise our son. Skagway is a great place. I'm not sure it needs a fancy hotel. I was tempted with the new house in Dyea but now I'm not so sure. I just want my family back." The muttering turned into angry bees all around my head. Judge Stanley banged his gavel three times. The bees went away.

"Do you have anything else to add?"

"Yes, your Honor. I know that any criminal things will have to wait until later but I have the bullet that shot my son. I comes out of a Winchester .22 long range rifle make in 1919. It was Model 1903."

"Are you a ballistics expert, Mrs. Jones?"

"No, your Honor. My husband had me get the bullet checked out. He gave it to me right before he was arrested."

"Objection! Everyone in Skagway has a gun! We hunt for a living. Hell, half of us have Winchesters that our fathers gave us!" Mr. Schumacher was on his feet. Judge Stanley banged his gavel. Hell is a place so I didn't use my special glossary. Mom might make me cut that word out before I become a great crime novelist.

"Mr. Schumacher. If you can't contain yourself then we will have Sheriff Tate put you in the cell next to your son. "Mr. Schumacher's face went purple. He sat down and looked at the floor. "Thank you for that information, Mrs. Jones. We will follow up on that information later. Do you have anything else to add?"

"No, your Honor."

"Please step down. I call Monica Greene to the stand." The town was whispering back and forth. Some of them pointed. They didn't want the gavel again. Mrs. Greene was holding my backpack tightly. I was rocking and writing. I was nervous to let go of my backpack, but she promised she would give it back. It was still dusty. She dressed up in a pretty blue dress. She looked really pretty. Aunt Edna was sitting next to Lawrence Henderson. The town called him Crazy Larry. He was the file clerk in the town hall for 40 years. After he retired, he quit shaving and ordered orange soda by the case. Every day he took the newspaper and sat in the café reading. He cut out special sections. He would take his pile and gently put the cuttings in a manila folder like they were pieces of the Bible. Then he would address the manila envelope to himself and put it in the mail.

Somebody said he had rows and rows of surplus file cabinets in his basement. Every day he picked up yesterday's news from the post office. Aunt Edna said once they tried to give it to him without the postmark on it but he threw a fit. He didn't trust computers. Aunt Edna insisted on calling him Lawrence. She always gave him a little smile. Larry always looked at the ground. I wondered if Crazy Larry was autistic. He didn't rock. Judge Stanley checked something on the last page of his legal pad. "Can you please give us your account of the situation, Mrs. Greene?"

"Yes, your Honor. In simple terms Ralph Schumacher lied to HVI, bullied the town and tried to destroy the reputation of Harry and his family." Mr. Schumacher's eyes were furious. His face turned a couple more shades of purple but he didn't say anything.

"Those are strong words, Mrs. Greene. Many years of planning have gone into this complex. Mr. Schumacher has faithfully served as the mayor of this town for many years." Judge Stanley said, looking over his glasses.

"I understand, your Honor. As Sheriff Tate said, Rudy asked to see me this morning. Rudy is a troubled, enraged young man. He told me he did it mostly to get back at his dad. He also did it because Mr. Schumacher was siphoning off construction materials. He kept doing it because Mr. Schumacher upset Rocky so much that first day. It turns out in his misguided attempt he wanted to defend Rocky. I mean Harold. Rudy got some buddies to help but he said he would explain everything else to his lawyer so he wouldn't get them in trouble."

"All of this is hearsay at the moment, Mrs. Greene."

"I understand. I explained that to Rudy."

"Please continue."

"Rudy said his dad was having secret conversations on the phone with people who didn't work for HVI. He was negotiating with different builders. From what Rudy overheard it sounds like we were all going to live in shacks in Dyea if we got anything at all. Worse than that, when Aunt Edna threatened the whole project by not selling her house, he sent people to pick on her. He even harassed her at work with phone calls. That's what happened to the carport. It was probably the cause of the fire. He's in the fire department and he didn't lift a finger the other night. On top of that, HVI thought they bought the entire property. It turns out they were misinformed." Now the HVI bigwigs were murmuring along with everyone in the room. The gavel banged three times. "You see, my great-great grandfather Frank Reid was one of the original surveyors for Skagway. When he started investigating Soapy Smith he found out that Soapy was planning more than just running a crooked town. He wanted to build a hotel in almost the exact location as HVI. To stop that, Frank Reid reserved lot 1070818981 as privately owned by our family. It's not much. Kind of like a private fishing dock. Skagway was just a glimmer. Nobody seemed to notice or care. Everyone wanted to get the gold."

"You have no proof!" Mr. Schumacher was on his feet again shouting and waving he chubby finger. The gavel came down really hard three times. Judge Stanley ordered Sheriff Tate to take Mr. Schumacher into custody and threatened to do the same thing to anyone else who decided to talk out of turn. Watching Sheriff Tate put the handcuffs on Mr. Schumacher and walk him out the back door made everybody really still. The whole place turned into church during a Christmas prayer. Mrs. Greene pulled out my backpack.

"The other night Harold snuck out of another house to help his family—like he did when he got shot." She smiled at me. Mom patted me on my knee. I kept writing. "He went to Aunt Edna's house to look for one of his notebooks. What he found was a hidden cellar built into the foundation. After the roof caved in and cracked it open he found the personal effects of Frank Reid. He had his wife promise not to tell anyone except family members. We've passed down that lot number from generation to generation."

"But why didn't that show up in the title search plans for HVI?" Judge Stanley asked.

"When so many buildings burnt down early on in Skagway the map was drawn and redrawn. Aunt Edna had Lawrence Henderson help her research the site. She trusted him with the only copy left to our family. About two years ago a fire started in Lawrence' basement and it burned up our 1898 copy. HVI could only prove ownership from 1919 but that' all they needed. This lot wasn't on it.

"This is quite a stretch, Mrs. Greene. I'm not sure how you can bring all that now when there has been three years of negotiating over the property."

"I understand. Aunt Edna and I also made a mistake. Even with the help of Mr. Henderson we couldn't trace that lot number through other records. The only thing we had was that one copy and it was faded. That was until today." Mrs. Greene pulled out the metal box. The crowd got tingly like I did. She opened the box and pulled out the diary of Frank Reid. "Just like Harold over there, Frank Reid kept notebooks. In his diary he made another small sketch of the area. That corner around the dock area wasn't just the lot number 1070818981. If you look here he put brackets around these numbers." She held it up for the Judge to look at it. He pulled his glasses closer and held the diary in his hand. He gently handed it back to her and nodded for her to continue. "He had his own little code inside his diary. His wife accidently added the number one where the brackets should be. The lot number was labeled [070818998]."

"This is all very fascinating but the diary will have to be professionally authenticated. Is there anything else?" Judge Stanley kept studying the diary, gently turning the pages.

"The only thing we have left to figure out is the number. It's on the map but it doesn't match anything for longitude or latitude. We don't understand it."

"It's the date!" I tried to use an inside voice to my mom but I've never really figured what that means. PIDU15. I yelled it.

"Excuse me, young man?" Judge Stanley banged his gavel.

"July 8, 1898. It's the day Frank Reid shot Soapy Smith." Mrs. Greene smiled.

"Why of course it is, young man. All things considered I'd have to say you put a new light on this matter." He banged his gavel again to stop the muttering. Suddenly you could hear the ticking of the old clock on the back wall as everyone waited. A man from HVI cleared his throat. Judge Stanley looked up and motioned for the man on the end to come up to the bench. He gently showed him the diary. He leaned sideways and showed the diary to Sheriff Tate who nodded. He whispered some things to the man from HVI who also nodded. Finally, he handed the diary back to Mrs. Greene while the man from HVI sat back down. Judge Stanley gathered his papers and tapped them three times. Now it was time for him to clear his throat. His shoulders slumped as he let out a sigh. "As the state appointed mediator in this hearing I find that further investigation is warranted into the different testimonies. The injunction to stop the construction of this hotel will be taken up at the scheduled formal court date in Juneau. Until all HVI activities are suspended."

Everyone in town stood up and cheered. Judge Stanley didn't bang his gavel. I clapped my hands over my ears. I yelled. Mom hugged me. She made it better. The ghost of Frank Reid saved the town.

Chapter 22

HVI cancelled the hotel. There wasn't a huge story paper in the story like when they arrested Dad. Dad came home and Mr. Schumacher went to jail. Mr. Schumacher was the only person in town with a Winchester Model 1903. It had special ammo that made it easy to trace back to the gun. It turned out Mr. Schumacher and Rudy were shooting at each other that night without knowing it. Mr. Schumacher thought I was one of the vandals. HVI settled with all the people in town. Mrs. Greene ended up with a settlement out of her lawsuit. HVI didn't want to be tied to Mr. Schumacher and the fire at Aunt Edna's house. When it was all said and done Mom and Dad owned Mr. Schumacher's beef jerky tourist shop. It turned out that Mr. Cooper was right. It really did taste like crap. Dad had Mrs. Warliss move her carvings into the store and added some other Tlingit touches. Rudy moved to Anchorage to live with his Aunt Frida and Uncle Bob. His mom died when he was three. I didn't get to say goodbye, but Mom said that maybe I could write him later.

Mrs. Greene moved up to Skagway for good. She expanded the city library so that more children would have things to do after school. She gave me a job organizing books after school. Life in Skagway is good for me. Everyone has two or three jobs. I carve bears for Mrs. Warliss and wash dishes for Grandma Tyler. I organize books for Mrs. Greene. I finally met her husband. He works on the big boats and is gone quite a bit out of the year. He was nice. I still write in my notebooks all the time. I rock all the time.

Especially at school and in crowds. My plan is still to become a famous crime novelist. Someday I'm going to let more people see my notebooks. Thanks for being my friend. Thanks for reading my notebooks.

About the Author

D.P. Johnson holds a Ph.D. in educational psychology with a concentration in reading. He has worked in public schools for the last 25 years and lives in rural Washington with his wife, son and a few alpacas. For more information about this book please email him at cavemoonpress@gmail.com